DATE DUE

GAYLORD		PRINTED IN U.S.A.

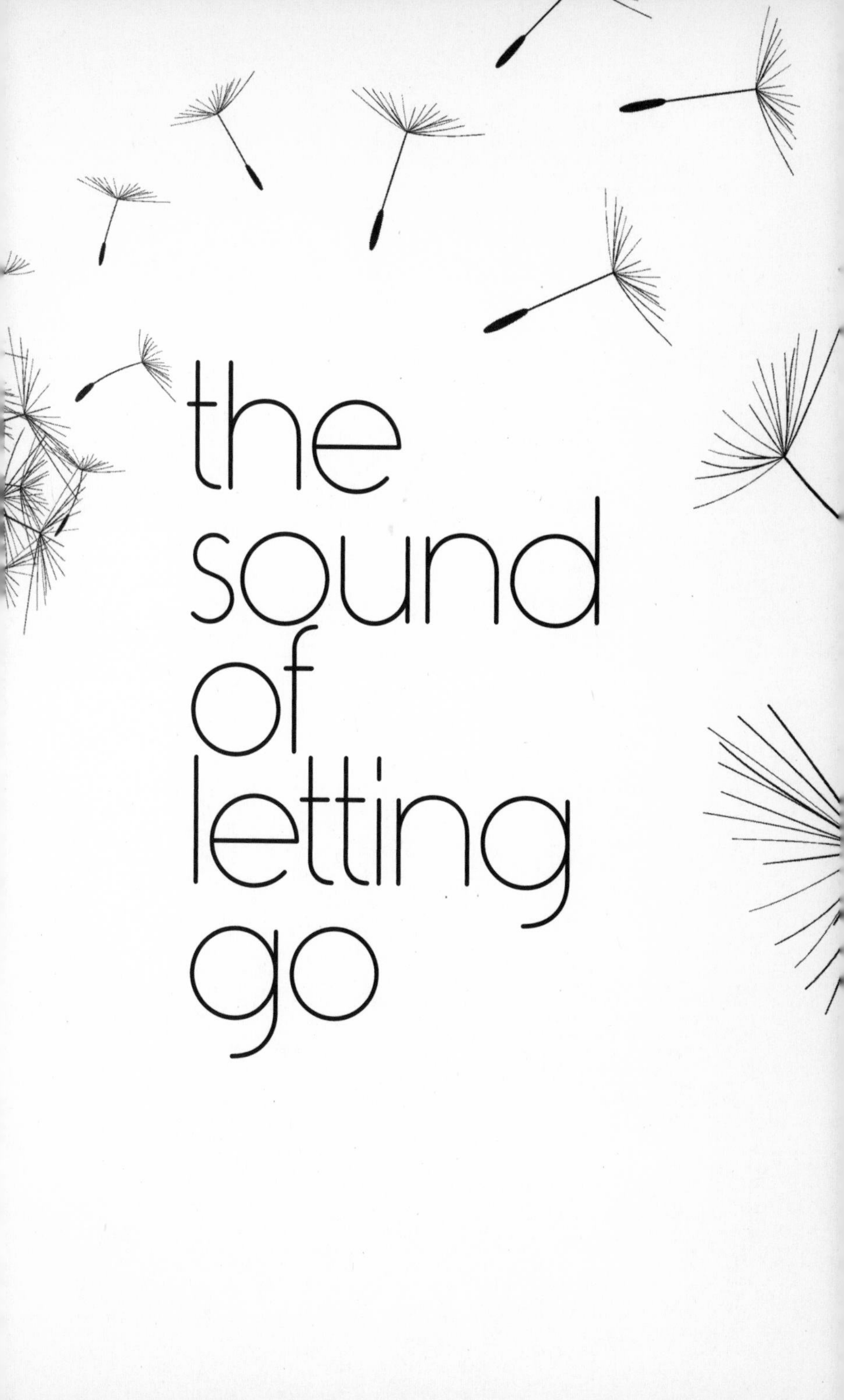
the
sound
of
letting
go

STASIA WARD KEHOE

the sound of letting go

VIKING
An Imprint of Penguin Group (USA)

VIKING
Published by the Penguin Group
Penguin Group (USA) LLC
375 Hudson Street
New York, New York 10014

USA * Canada * UK * Ireland * Australia
New Zealand * India * South Africa * China

penguin.com
A Penguin Random House Company

First published in the United States of America by Viking, an imprint of Penguin Group (USA) LLC, 2014

LIBRARY OF CONGRESS CATALOGING-IN-PUBLICATION DATA
Kehoe, Stasia Ward. date–
The sound of letting go / by Stasia Ward Kehoe.
pages cm
Summary: At seventeen, Daisy feels imprisoned by her brother Steven's autism and its effects and her only escape is through her trumpet into the world of jazz, but when her parents decide to send Steven to an institution she is not ready to let him go.
ISBN 978-0-670-01553-5 (hardcover)
[1. Novels in verse. 2. Autism—Fiction. 3. Trumpet—Fiction. 4. Jazz—Fiction. 5. High schools—Fiction. 6. Schools—Fiction. 7. Family problems—Fiction.] I. Title.
PZ7.5.W24Sou 2014
[Fic]—dc23
2013013098

Printed in the USA Set in Spectrum MT Std

10 9 8 7 6 5 4 3 2 1

For Thomas, Mak, Sam, Jack,

and Kevin.

Always.

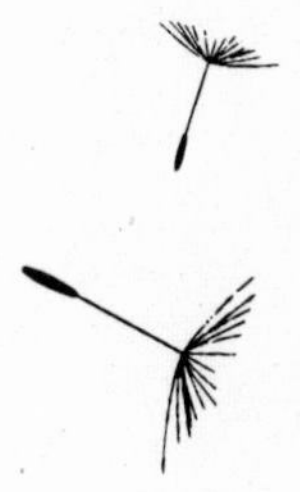

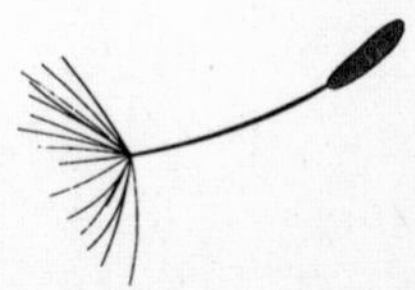

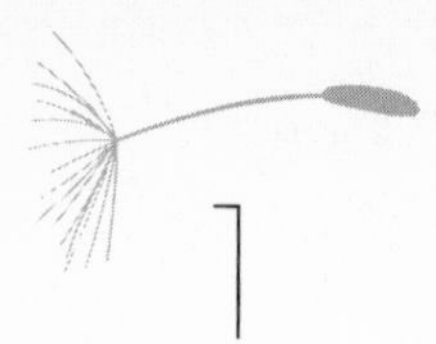

1

Dave Miller grins in my direction.
At least, I think
his easy-eyed, right-cheek-dimpled expression
is meant for me.

It's hard to be certain, since we are separated
by the fingerprinted interior window that divides
my band room refuge from the chaotic dissonance
of the rest of Evergreen High.

Dave was my best friend in kindergarten.
We split jelly (no peanut butter) sandwiches together,
told our parents that we'd marry
and build a house, someday, in Dave's backyard.
But life isn't kindergarten, and by now,
junior year of high school,
we live on different social planets,
our orbits rarely intersecting,
though sometimes, in the morning,
he's there outside the band room
making my stomach flutter,
making me want a peanut-butter-free jelly sandwich.

I wonder what sort of smile would telegraph the reply,
If-you-are-looking-at-me-hey-there-but-if-you-are-not-
I-don't-mind.
Whatever it is, I hope that's my expression
as I pack up my trumpet,
smooth my hand over the once-black case
now customized with a zillion jazz-musician,
classic-album, instrument art stickers I've made
using mom's scrapbooking gadgets

because my mother keeps things organized.
Our lives in labeled albums,
our showpiece house in designer paint colors
vacuumed, swept, so pretty that if you just looked
you might want to come inside.
But if you listened,
you'd hear another story:
incomprehensible wailing,
shouting, urgent phone calls,
crying. You'd want to ask if a monster
lived in our house.

I am not sure how I'd answer.

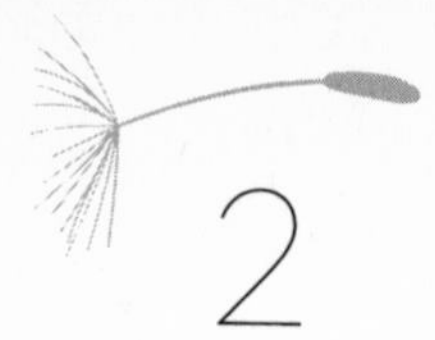

2

I snap the buckles,
hoist my backpack over one shoulder,
slide my trumpet case up onto a band room shelf.
I'll retrieve it after school.

"Busy tonight, Daisy?"
Dave catches me at the door.

I resist the instinctive *why?*
and say, "Not really."

"A bunch of us are going to The Movie House.
Wanna come?"

Dave's golden-brown eyes hold me,
his hopeful voice a beckoning bell

silenced by the drum crash of reality.
Wednesday is one of Mom's yoga nights.
A night I watch Steven.

"I—I think I'll have too much homework for that."

3

Heart skidding, I walk down the hall to homeroom,
eyes pointed resolutely forward, resisting
the urge to glance back, see if Dave is watching.
I slide my backpack off my shoulder, straighten my spine,
give my hair a casual, carefree shake, just in case.

"The Movie House," I whisper through near-motionless lips.
I have this habit of sometimes saying words out loud,
narrating my life as I wish it could be,
pretending the pounding in my chest is because I am,
secretly, a spy girl or mad scientist,
that my reason for scurrying home, turning down Dave,
is something more exotic than unpleasant.

I let my imagination wander to the possibility of *yes*.
In my mind, I sit at The Movie House beside Dave
and he puts his hand gently over mine on the armrest
that separates us,
and it doesn't feel anything like our old sandbox high fives,
and he isn't the detention-garnering slacker he's become
but the astronaut-engineer-firefighter he used to portray

when he wore a near-perpetual chocolate-milk mustache
and hair buzzed short by his dad, like a soldier's.

"Wednesday at The Movie House"
could be the title for an album,
something brassy, instrumental, full of hope.
And that makes me smile a little,
thinking of music inside my head despite my pulsing regret
for saying no.

4

At three fifteen, I haul my feet
to the parking lot, drag
my bags along the ground, not caring
if the rip, tug, pull,
the bump-scratch of trumpet case
grazing asphalt
slows me down.

It is hard to go home.
Sometimes I think I'd join any band, rehearse any song,
for the chance to be away from that place an extra hour.

If I called Mom, asked,
she'd probably let me go to The Movie House tonight.
But I can't do that to her.

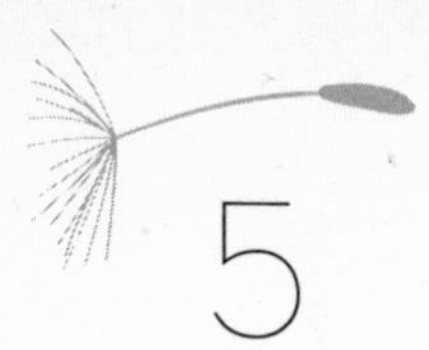

5

"I'm back!" I announce not too loudly,
slipping the house key back into my jeans pocket.
"Mom?"

I get no reply, but head to the kitchen anyway.

As I pass the table, Steven catches my arm
in a grip that's gotten tighter,
rougher, since he turned thirteen.
His feet keep growing.
His face is getting pimply.
He is starting to look like a man.

"Hi, Daisy."
Mom is wearing her "Kiss the Cook" apron
over a blue-and-white yoga ensemble.

"Is that new?" I ask
as I pull my arm from its vice-hold,
already glad I didn't disappoint her
by asking to escape tonight.

It's still two hours until yoga
and she's already dressed to go.

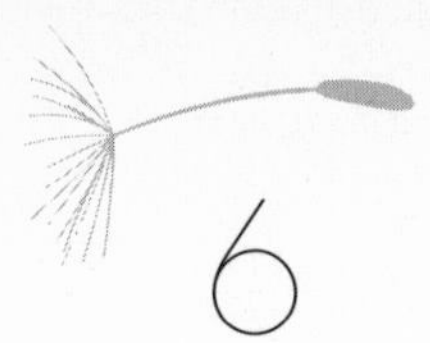

6

"We made chocolate chip cookies." Mom unties her apron.
"Would you mind if I left a little early?
A few other yoga-moms are meeting for tea before class."

"Go ahead," I say,
sitting down at the kitchen table across from my brother.

Mom puts a cookie on my paper plate,
places another in Steven's hand.
I do not like warm cookies.
I prefer to wait until the chocolate chips
have gotten cool, firm, and the cookie a little crispy.
But I take a bite.

Steven taps his cookie against his lips,
the bottom of his nose,
then he pushes it into his mouth,
crumbs dropping onto the table.
The cookie finished, he settles into a familiar pose—
head cocked to the left,

gazing vaguely upward as if the ceiling reveals secrets
only he can see.
I watch the energy transfer to Steven's plump fingers:
Elbows drawn tight against his belly,
he moves his forearms slowly,
not the agile, winglike flapping that stereotypes autistics
on television
but a cruel series of arduous passes—
palm over back of hand . . . palm over back of hand . . .
His knuckles are calloused, reddish from wear.

Mom bustles around the kitchen.
"The casserole should come out at five thirty.
Dad's working late again,
but he'll be home to put Steven to bed.
I'll give him his meds before I go."

"Want to go watch TV, Steven?" I ask.

Nothing.

I stand up. "TV in the family room, Steven?"

Beat . . . Beat . . .

"No-ahhh." His flat, tuneless half-word/half-moan

instantly stops Mom's sweeping.

"How about Blokus?"
She pulls the box from the kitchen island,
slides it before Steven.

Plastic pieces tumble onto the table.
I have "played" Blokus with Steven many times;
our game rule is simply that I watch him
align the square chips
in single-colored rows until the board is full.
Sometimes we do it three times or more,
Steven's hands wringing
as he contemplates the colors, almost never acknowledging
that I am sitting across from him
or that he feels any satisfaction in completing a row.

"There." Mom nods her head
as Steven begins to focus on the game.
"You'll be fine."

"Yeah."
I calculate the breadth of Steven's shoulders,
now wider than mine;
count the hours
between now and Dad coming home to take over;

and I am only a little afraid
of the night.

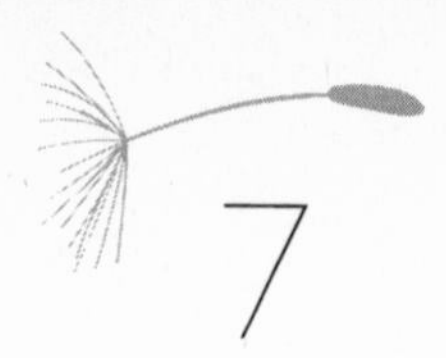

7

In the morning,
the wails are my alarm clock.
Steven does not like to take a shower, brush his teeth.
Most of all, he hates to put on deodorant.

I wait under the quilt
as the sun teases through the slats in the window blinds,
until thudding footsteps on the stairs report
the second floor has been emptied of everyone but me.

Then I haul myself out of bed, tired, as always,
from a late night of homework and trumpet practice
that can only begin
after one of my parents has come home to take over Steven.
I rub my eyes, trying to remember
a morning when I woke up feeling rested,
a day that wasn't a constant strain of worries,
a time when I didn't care
about time.

Breakfast is another terse routine of favorite foods,
Mom's constant monologue of calming words,
restating the day's plan,
asking Dad random questions about the news, the weather,
as if we lived in an ordinary house,
could take pleasure in morning conversation.

I ghost my way through the kitchen,
pour cereal from the nearest box to hand
into a clean bowl, slosh in milk,
eat at the kitchen island, while Mom, Dad, and Steven
circle the table with their family farce.

"Today at school, we're not going to hit anyone,
right, Steven?
We are going to sit nicely in our seat and not hit, right?"
Mom tries to keep her voice steady.
Dad lets out a long breath from behind his paper.

We are living on the verge of Steven's dismissal
from his current special-needs public school program,
where he has begun to smack the teachers almost daily,
grab at the wrists of his female classmates
if they pass too closely by his desk.
Our growing fear of life with him intensifies
with every evening phone call

from the special ed program director,
with every e-mail documenting "discrepancies"
between his "individualized education plan"
(IEP, to those in our world)
and what they now believe he can accomplish
in their classroom.

In the window of hours while Steven is away "learning,"
Mom keeps our house
a showpiece of calm colors,
creates scrapbooks full of deceptively happy memories,
and scours the Internet
for a doctor, a diet, a drug that can help retrieve
her once adorable, odd little boy
from inside the puffed overlay of oily, angry man-child,
or at least keep him safe,
keep us all safe.

"Gotta go. Early practice this morning."
I am out the door before Dad blames Mom
for Steven's untied shoes
and announces his usual plan to be home late from work.
Before Mom coaxes Steven into his jacket, Dad's car.

Mom has long since given up
on getting real affection from Steven,

but there's this look on her face
every time she stands in front of Dad
as he picks up his briefcase, buckles his watch,
grabs his keys,
but doesn't kiss her good-bye.

I always try to be gone before that.

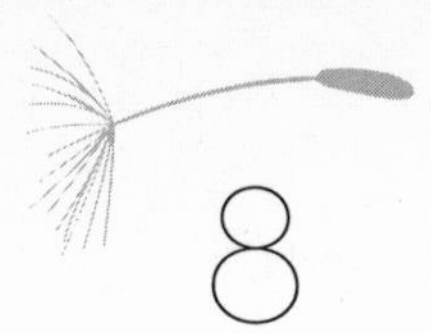

8

I pull my car into the school lot, look for Dave's Fiesta.
It is mostly black, with a red hood and one red rear door
salvaged, I guess, from another ancient Ford.
It has not yet arrived at its usual parking spot
near the row of maple trees on the far side of the asphalt.
I'm not sure if it's disappointment
or the moist fall chill that makes me shiver,
but I zip my fleece jacket
before I grab my backpack and trumpet case,
squint up at the hazy sky,
head for the front doors of Evergreen High.

Jazz Ensemble,
7:15 to 8:10 a.m.,
Tuesday through Friday:
best 220 minutes of my week.

Nine boys, four girls:
trumpets, saxophones, clarinets,
a trombone, a bass, drums;

melodies, rhythms, riffs, and improvs;
occasional bad notes, squawks, laughter.

No wailing.

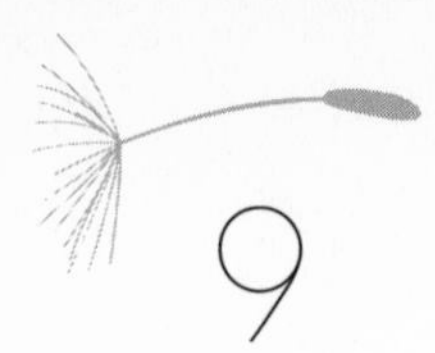

9

There are more guys than girls in the jazz world,
next to no lady trumpeters (oh, there are a few).
But it doesn't matter because, for me,
jazz trumpet is all about one guy:
Miles Davis.
He made this famous album in 1959
called *Kind of Blue*,
which is kind of, always,
how I feel.

That album gets into your bones,
goes and goes;
starts, hesitates, reaches out, feels
for the music, the sound, the thing you want to change.
Always grasping for the unattainable makes you
kind of excited,
kind of sorry.

10

Mr. Orson taps his music stand.
We're all waiting to get started
because today is Thursday: Jam Session.
We'll play through tons of music, hardly stopping,
just letting the music roll, feeling good, letting go.

"Before we start today,
I'd like you all to welcome Callum O'Casey."

"Er, um, it's just Cal," comes a quiet Irish brogue
from thin lips, moving so slightly
it takes a moment to realize he's the one speaking.
"Just Cal for short."

The other three jazz girls sit up at the sound of his accent,
look sharp toward the saxophone section.
Cal-for-short's long legs stretch into the aisle.
As he speaks, a dark pink blush starts at his ears,
spreads to his fresh, pale cheeks.
He's wearing untucked brown plaid flannel and holey jeans.
His baritone sax, slightly tarnished, dull yellow metal,

lies across his lap, braced so lightly in his hand
it seems like he doesn't even need to hold on.

"Good to have a bari again, *Cal*,"
Mr. Orson says with emphasis.
"Had one graduate last year and we've been missing it."

And we're off.
It's November,
which means jazz versions of Christmas carols,
plus the Ellington piece we're learning
for the Northeast Battle of the Bands competition.

Cal-for-short can read music, man,
because that bari is already coming in strong,
giving the numbers that deep undertow thrum
they've apparently been missing,
though I didn't really know it
until the bari came back.

11

Lots of guys and all the other girls
stick around after practice to welcome the new player.
But through the glass, I see the back of Dave Miller's head,
so I close my case, stash it on a shelf, dash into the hall.

"Hey!" I give him a shove.

"Hey back. You missed a good movie last night.
Serial killer with an ax really messed up a town."

"Sounds like Oscar material." I smile
an I-am-smart-but-not-too-smart-
for-you-to-think-I'm-sexy smile.
At least, I hope I do.

"After, we drove down to the pits.
Belden brought some great home brew."

Dave and Josh Belden and the rest of those guys
hang out with the girls who wear bars of black liner

underneath their eyes, who jangle
with boot and belt buckles, chainy stuff.
Their place:
a circle of fire pits near the picnic tables at the town park.
They've carpeted it with cigarette butts,
amped up the tables with neatly carved expletives
and the occasional X-hearts-Y proclamation.

I do not wear heavy makeup,
have nothing pierced besides my ears.
My clothes are generic except
for the Sharpie-drawn flowers and music-note stamps
that enhance the canvas of the Keds I wear every day.
I don't drink,
don't deface property beyond stickering my trumpet case.
But there's something about the badassness of Dave Miller
that makes me sorry I missed The Movie House,
wonder about the taste of Belden's home brew.

With a start I realize that I've drifted away,
feel my eyes on Dave's face,
my expression surely more wistful than sexy.
He is looking at me curiously.
I've been silent too long,
dreaming last night had been different,

that I'd been with Dave.
Though now, with him standing in front of me,
I am a total idiot.

"Um, yeah, home brew. How do you make that?"

Dave scratches his already-mussed hair,
which somehow makes it look even better.
"I didn't make the stuff. I just—"

"Oh, never mind. Sounds like a fun night."

I start wishing I was in a slasher film,
that someone with an ax would come
and strike me down right now
before I can say anything MORE stupid than I have already.
I am definitely one of the characters they'd kill off
early in those movies. Right now, it'd be a relief.

Instead of an ax, it's a sound that comes to my rescue:
the warning bell for homeroom.

"Well, guess I gotta go," I say.

"Yeah," he says.

"Um, it was nice talking with you."
My mouth won't stop moving.

He gives a little laugh, calls over his shoulder,
"You've always been a funny one, Daisy Meehan."

I watch the back of him for far too long.

12

"Thank you for gracing us with your presence,
Ms. Meehan." Mrs. Pendleton glances up from her desk.

"Sorry." I duck my head and slide into my seat,
embarrassed by my staring-at-Dave-Miller delay.
I'm a good student, rarely late,
and I doubt she'll mark me tardy.

"Students, I'd like you to welcome . . ."

And homeroom is another rendezvous
with "Um, er, just Cal" O'Casey,
who seems to be appearing everywhere I am.

From the seat in front of me, my best friend, Justine,
turns around to shoot an oh-my-God,
hottest-accent-ever look of awe.

"He's in jazz band," I whisper.

Her expression morphs into raging envy.

"I'm gonna learn to play the triangle," she whispers back.

I giggle. Justine can always make me laugh.
Even when I've been up half the night, alone in my room,
listening to the music-less sounds of Steven smacking walls,
my parents fighting over whether to restrain or medicate,
then, if it ends, their clumping staggers down the stairs
to dose themselves with wine.

"Care to share the joke, girls?" Mrs. Pendleton says.

"Oh, I was just saying that maybe someone
should buddy up with Cal,
help him find his way around the school."

Another thing about Justine: she's got a pair.

"And that's funny?" the teacher persists.

"Depends on the buddy, I suppose."
Justine smiles with mock sweetness.

No girls like Mrs. Pendleton.
She is too pretty, too young;
her firefighter husband is too cool, too cute;

and she steals the attention of too many junior boys
from us junior girls.
Not that it's her fault.
She's all ambitious young teacher,
struggling to awaken us country bumpkins
to the wonders of environmental science.
There's a picture of Mr. Pendleton on her desk,
and I've caught her texting him during class
on more than one occasion.

I look over at Cal O'Casey,
wondering if he's fallen victim to the Pendleton charm,
but he is looking down
at his brown, lace-up shoes,
which might be stylish in Ireland
but are simply geekishly adorable in Jasper, New Hampshire.
He may not be ready
for Justine's American sense of humor.

"That's a nice offer, Ms. Jenkins,"
Mrs. Pendleton says to Justine.
"Would you care to be said 'buddy'?"

"I, um—that's okay." Cal drags his eyes up from the floor.
"I think I can manage a'right."

A couple of girls actually swoon over his last, Irish word.

Justine sticks her chin out, her eyes set.
I know she's willing her pale, freckled skin not to blush.

I make a mental note that, accent or not,
Callum O'Casey is a bit of a jerk.

13

Some days I just can't bear all those stories they tell
in Advanced Placement United States History—
they call it A-PUSH, like that makes it cooler.
It doesn't.
Not that I disrespect the Declaration of Independence,
the Constitution, all those rebels, free thinkers,
George Washington, Ben Franklin,
Thomas Jefferson, Andrew Jackson.
I get it. They wanted freedom.

Well I do, too.

But you can't really have freedom
without making someone else a kind of prisoner,

can you?

14

Justine and I sit at the same table every lunch period,
where we're joined by a few band friends of mine,
some drama types she knows,
and the occasional Extremely Serious Schoolboy—
the kind she and I seem to attract— the ones who rule
the Student Council and Entrepreneurship Club.

Today the lunch is turkey and gravy,
which is gross to look at but which I secretly like.
I like the fake mashed potatoes,
made from hot milk and potato flakes,
a product that would never see
the perfect interior paint colors of our house.
I like the tiny chunks of turkey,
the tasteless peas, and the whitish sauce.
I like the cookie that comes on the side:
cool, nearly stale, chocolate chips firm.
I like not having to think, to choose;
just slop it on my plate
and I'm all good, thank you.

Today, Ned Hoffman from
Students Against Drunk Driving
is making eyes at Justine.
I poke my fork into the smooth white mound of lunch,
look across the aisle. Callum O'Casey is being lit upon
by three blonde cheerleaders,
I guess because his accent charms, because his red hair
stands out in the crowd.
Though I kind of think they wouldn't let him
get into their pants—an honor
reserved for the Varsity Football starting line.

I lean away from Ned, who is earnestly telling Justine
about some flower sale fund-raiser
attached to the upcoming Black-and-White Dance,
strain to catch fragments of Cal's description
of his cultural exchange program:
how lucky he was to be allowed to come,
even though the school year had already started;
how he'll be staying with the Ackermans,
his host family, until June. Just like in homeroom,
his expression is a little strained, his cheeks a little pink.
He seems surprised and confused
by the attention he's getting. I guess he doesn't know
how exotic he seems here in Jasper.

"Well, I think you should sell pink roses, too.
Red is just so . . . dramatic,"
Justine says loudly, returning my attention to our table.
"Don't you think, Daisy?"

"Um, yeah." I nod, remind myself
that Cal was rude to my friend—who, right now,
might need a rescue from her determined suitor,
and who loves things that are pink.
"Pink flowers are terrific."

"See?" Justine's flashing eyes refocus on Ned.
Instructions about what girls like pour from her lips,
keeping any more of Cal's words from reaching my ears.

I close my eyes and imagine the music of Cal's brogue,
the lilt
the tempo of an Irish folk tune,
the kind my parents tell me they used to listen to
when they first fell in love—
as if they are in love anymore.

15

My parents tell the stories
of their courtship, their marriage, their life before kids
to me—only me—never Steven.
I alone hold their history in my brain.
I am the only child in the house
who mourns the loss of their romance,
the only one who can hear in the tones of their voices
longing,
rejection,
apology,
a broken connection between hearts,
between people.

The bell rings.
The din around me quiets.
The sounds of Ireland empty from my brain.

"See you later." Ned, looking mildly defeated,
stands up and heads for the cafeteria door.

Justine and I look across the aisle
to where Cal O'Casey has gallantly stacked
two girls' trays beneath his own,
getting set to clear their table.

16

I am the keeper of secrets,
I think, as Justine shoves tinfoil into her paper lunch bag,
confesses: "I wanted to die
when that boy shut me down in homeroom.
I mean, what a jerk.
Couldn't he have just taken my hospitality?
I can't believe I thought he was cute
when he first walked into the room."

"You didn't." I try to comfort her.
We walk toward the exit.
"It was just when he spoke. That accent's pretty hot.
But he's not so cute."

"You're the best friend ever." She smiles.
Usually, she waits beside me
through the dump-your-hot-lunch-tray line,
then we head together to our fifth-period classes:
hers, choir; mine, concert band—
oh yeah, the dynamic duo of coolness.

But today, I see surprise in her eyes; she's gone with a wave.

"You've got a good appetite for somebody so thin."
In a flash, I understand Justine's departure:
Dave Miller is behind me,

standing so close his elbow brushes mine,
which makes my guts jump, my tongue go stupid.

"Been a long time since breakfast," I say.
Not my worst reply at all. I steal a look at his tray,
as empty as mine.
"Admit it," I tease, "you *like* those mashers!"

He drops his fork into the bin,
slides his tray onto the metal clearing shelf,
raises his arms up mockingly.
"Guilty as charged, officer.
I have high-class taste, just like you!"

"Um, would you move it!"
Ashleigh Anderson demands, doesn't ask.
She's heeled and blonde,
behind us with Cal in tow, who's quiet again,
looking down.

I shove my tray onto the shelf
and glare at them both on Justine's behalf.
"C'mon, Dave," I snark.
"Let's get going to our gourmet cooking class."

Surprisingly, he follows.

17

"So, you coming?" he asks as we clear the cafeteria door.

"Coming where?"

"I'm gonna go have an after-lunch relax out back."
He grins that shaggy Dave Miller grin.

"I can't. I have concert band."

"You've already done band once today.
Fifteen minutes. They won't miss you."

Two nose-ringed girls pass by us at the lockers,
wave to Dave.
I imagine the "out back" he's headed for:
a smoky, not-college-bound,
what-the-heck-we've-got-detention-anyway
stand of bleachers not far from the dumpsters.

My trumpet is waiting for me on the band room shelf.
Concert band music is not nearly as much fun to play as jazz.

The group is larger, more amateur. Still,
the flutter in my heart fizzles.

Am I miserable as I say,
"No, I am first chair of the trumpets,"
and scurry away?

Am I miserable when, after school,
I watch his Ford Fiesta squeal out of the parking lot,
then turn my Subaru in the opposite direction?

"Dream a Little Dream of Me," from the Louis Armstrong
and Ella Fitzgerald album in my car's CD player,
serenades me down Main Street,
past Bouchard's Flower and Gift Shoppe.

Small-town folks don't like chain stores.
We flock through Bouchard's horseshoe-shaped doors
even though the place is owned by Andy Bouchard,
who took up with Dave's mom, broke up the Miller family.
It was she who encouraged him to put in the coffee bar.

But other peoples' affairs
aren't anybody's business in Jasper,
and we all prefer Bouchard's Special Blend
to what the baristas pour

into those franchise-familiar
green-and-white cups one town over.

New Englanders are proud people.
We don't talk much about what's going on
behind other people's doors.
Nobody's business but their own.
We don't talk about everyone's secrets,
even though we know them.

What happens inside my house is nobody else's business, too.
But I know Dave knows my family's story as well as I know
why he'll never be spotted drinking a latte at Bouchard's.
So I hope he understands, or at least suspects
that I'm dreaming of him
even as I drive toward my quiet neighborhood,
down my well-landscaped street,
right on time.

18

I live in a house of metronomes
ticking back and forth, back and forth,
with no better purpose
than to keep the tempo from changing; not
to guide musicians in a song, to create a symphony,
but simply to keep the chaos always nipping at our toes
from biting off our legs.

Mom's yoga is Monday, Wednesday, Friday,
so Thursday is a good night to get homework done.
I read passels of A-PUSH,
conjugate French verbs in the pluperfect tense,
ruing my stubborn refusal to take Spanish,
my idiot argument that I wanted to read
Victor Hugo's *Les Misérables* in its original language.

Sometimes I feel guilty
that I resent learning French when Steven
can barely form a handful of words.
His sounds, when he makes them, are atonal,
uninflected, as if he cannot hear himself.

For Steven, sound is an enemy.
Noises too high, too loud, lead him to self-harm—
twisting his palms until they're bloody,
smacking his head against walls, floors.
And so he has silenced the rest of us in this house.
We tiptoe, whisper, exist in an even, steady cadence
that belies the sadness, the frustration,
even the laughter we might release
behind some other front door.

French finished,
I head to the basement for trumpet practice,
so it won't disturb Steven.

When he was younger,
he seemed able to tolerate more music.
I played my trumpet in the family room, and Mom
used to harbor dreams
that he would become one of those savant-like people
who, despite myriad challenges, had a talent to share—
a gift to give the world.
Back then, our house was filled with paintbrushes,
crayons, tambourines, and recorders,
and when Steven drew on the walls
or smashed an instrument to bits,
she would just grab a sponge or broom and try again.

Now, the toys have been put away
with the good china and sharp steak knives,
the picture frames and crystal vases.

Now it's only once in a while that I try playing for him:
gentle tunes with narrow ranges, repetitions—
"Row, Row, Row Your Boat" and "Frère Jacques"—
easy, steady notes.
But on those rare occasions,
I don't think I am just imagining
that I see his face muscles relax, his body still.
I picture his mind escaping to some faraway place
where he can communicate,
grow up,
understand, and maybe
really love us.

That face tells me when I've played a perfect note.

19

Friday breakfast
again at the island,
three others sitting at that table.
Toaster waffles cut in nine precise pieces
to please Steven, comfort him;
just the right smear of butter,
perfect soaking of syrup,
and Mom, grinning, saying "Isn't this a lovely morning,"
as if the words, her lyrics for the day, could make it so;
as if the morning could be anything more
than another preamble, another overture
to a future none of us can predict or understand.

Sometimes I close my eyes and see the four of us in it.
More often, the image is just Mom and Steven and me.
Dad has gone off and found someone else to love,
someone without the baggage,
the pain we bring him.
Mom goes to yoga every night
and I am still there, watching Steven,
waiting for my own life to begin.

I've got to escape this place.

20

Can music people read each other's minds
from all the way across town?
Know today is the day someone needs to be rescued?

Mr. Orson catches me after jazz band—
which is good because I don't see Dave Miller
in the hall, so my mood would've sunk
if it weren't for his hand on my shoulder.

"Daisy, I'd like you to take a look at this."
The school music director puts a booklet in my hand.
"It's an application to the Overton Music Academy's
Summer Jazz Intensive.
If you're interested,
I'd be happy to write you a recommendation."

I know the place. Kids from that summer program
get accepted to Juilliard—
the high note of collegiate music programs—
get invited to play with national orchestras,
score recording contracts . . .

I know, too, that it's in Pennsylvania,
enough miles from home
to make visits from my family practically impossible.

I imagine a new future scenario, another trio:
Mom, Dad, and Steven making do for the summer
while I am in Philadelphia,
City of Brotherly Love,
home of the great Ben Franklin of A-PUSH fame.
Suddenly even history is more appealing.

"I know you've got a challenging family situation,"
Mr. Orson interjects into my reverie.
"If it's not something you could—"

"Oh, no. I could. I mean, I would love to apply.
Overton looks amazing." I fan the pages in my hand,
barely glancing at the details, the words, the price—
at anything beyond the promise
of a rest,
a few weeks away from home,
a break from the cursed routines
that serve nobody but Steven.

21

In homeroom, Justine puts one earbud in my ear,
keeps the other for herself.
We sit with our heads together, listening
to Billy Joel's classic "Piano Man" on her iPod—
she loves good lyrics even if they're decades old.
It's a song about a washed-up musician
who's never made it anywhere,
but people ask him, always, for a song.

And it's like another sign, another "don't be like that,"
egging me on, telling me to apply to Overton
even though, despite what I told Mr. Orson,
a note of doubt is already flattening my optimistic tune.

Would Dad let me apply and leave Mom with no one
to spell her for yoga—hell, for a trip to the grocery store—
since our last willing babysitter quit
after Steven's new teenager-strong legs
kicked a hole through the front hall closet door?

If I asked them together,

would Mom come to my defense while Dad was all
too-much-money-too-much-time-too-much-stress
until I was the too-much that drove him off
beyond the office late nights,
weekend golf outings, ever-longer "runs"?

"What is it?" Justine asks.

I am sitting beside her,
index finger still pressed against the one earbud,
listening to silence since the song has ended,
the final bell has just rung,
and Mrs. Pendleton, in an offensively flattering blue skirt,
is walking up to her desk.

I am not ready to say the word *Overton* out loud,
so I just giggle,
"Oops, I was thinking about music,"
which is always kind of true.

Justine snorts. Her eyes stray to the evil Cal O'Casey,
whom I can only hate so much
because he plays his saxophone like nobody's business
and never complains
about having all the crappy bari lines.

In fact, it seems to me his biggest flaw
is that he says mostly nothing, asks for nothing,
refuses help.
If it weren't for his brogue attracting so much attention,
I think he'd manage to disappear.

22

I can't believe I'm sorry
that in history class we're gunning toward the Civil War.
Now I want to roll back to October,
revisit the first Constitutional Convention,
see the Liberty Bell in glorious, glorious Pennsylvania.

They've put poor Cal in this class, though
his entire knowledge of American history seems to consist
of insights into the psyche of mad King George.
Justine glances at his bewildered face,
whispers, "Bet now he wishes he had me for a tutor."
That's what you get from the logistics of a small-town
public school:
only two foreign language options
and an Irish kid drowning in A-PUSH.

"That Ellington piece was somethin' this morning."
Cal catches me and Justine at the door after class.
His words aren't a question,
and I don't know how he wants me to reply.
"Think we have a shot at the Battle of the Bands finals?"

That's a question with an easy answer.
Even though I think Cal plays almost as well as me,
and he's right,
the Ellington piece sounded amazing this morning.
"There are lots of entrants," I say.
"We're up against private schools and big-city programs.
So the odds aren't great."

"Music is tough like that.
So much about competitions, getting accepted places.
Winning. More like football, er, soccer,
than most people know."

"That's true." I feel my face crinkle into a smile.

"Enough music talk." Justine links her arm with mine.
"It's time for lunch."

23

A bowl of frighteningly red soup sits before me,
its tomato base enriched with every meat and vegetable
that didn't get used up earlier in the week.
Good old "Friday Soup Surprise"
doesn't taste as bad as you'd think.
I eat hot lunch every day,
not just because I'm too lazy to pack
but because it sets me free from Chez Autistic Frère
(that's partly French, thank you)
a few minutes faster.
I crumble eight packs of generic saltine crackers
into the ruby swill,
add pepper.
Not so bad.

"I don't know how you can eat that!"
Justine pushes mandarin oranges around her plate.

"Just close your eyes," I tell her.

"Like you were doing in homeroom?

What was that look on your face?
Dreaming about Dave Miller, maybe?"

"Not only."
I push the Overton brochure across the lunch table.

"Oh. My. God. You have to go!" she squeals.

"Go where?" Ned, in a light gray shirt and khakis,
sits down beside her.

"Just some band thing." I take the brochure back,
grateful for Justine's "talk later" gaze.
"How's choir?"

She rolls her eyes. "You know. Christmas carols."

"I love Christmas carols," Ned says.

"That so, Little Drummer Boy?"
It's Dave Miller,
not sitting down or anything but, empty tray in hand,
kind of lingering near where we are.

A holy-cow-Dave-has-come-by-my-table-
two-days-running
(also partly a wow-Dave-really-doesn't-like-Ned) giggle

escapes my lips along with a wet shard of cracker,
which I smear away quickly with the back of my hand.

"At least I like something."
Ned lifts his longish nose into the air.
His Adam's apple slides up the front of his thin neck.

"I like *some* things." Dave grins
and nods his head at my bowl of soup. "Not that."

"How do you know if you don't try it?" I ask,
even managing a flick of the hair, a hint of tease in my tone.

"Isn't that the question?" He looks at me pointedly.
I think of The Movie House, the pits,
the places to which Dave has invited me,
the places I haven't gone,
the things I've imagined about him. I swallow.
The acid residue of tomato broth stings my throat.

"Okay," Justine pipes into the silence,
"we all like something. We all hate the red soup.
Except for Daisy.
You gonna sit down, Dave?"

I turn my lips
into what I hope is a careless yet inviting smile, eyes on Dave.

He grins back but shakes his head.
"Think I'll go catch a few rays of sunshine
before the bell."

Justine and Ned and I follow him with our eyes
as he tosses his soda can in the recycle bin,
deposits his tray, saunters out the cafeteria door.

"Good that you stayed with us, Daisy.
That guy is such a jerk," Ned says.

There is almost too much to parse:
the implied "us" of Justine-and-Ned.
Ned approving of my actions in that parent-like way,
calling Dave a jerk, even though Ned was the one
flaunting snoot-in-air attitude.

"You should know, Ned," is my retort
as a memory flashes into my mind
of a day in second grade:
After using the bathroom,
I accidentally tucked my skirt into my polka-dot tights,
exposing my underpants
and a full view of the backs of my legs
to the entire class.
Halfway back to my seat, I noticed Ned giggling.

When he caught my eye, he looked down,
saying nothing.
It was Dave who stood up from his chair
(without asking Ms. Martin, our teacher's, permission),
walked over to me, and whispered,
"Hey, better fix your skirt."

Dave didn't get in trouble.
At that moment Ms. Martin looked up from her desk,
saw, understood,
came over to my desk,
and wordlessly straightened things out.

Now Dave is always tardy, breaking rules,
while Ned fund-raises for our school by selling flowers,
and I don't know who is right and who is wrong,
only that, if you lived in my house,
attended Autism Family Support Group meetings,
you'd find it hard to be self-righteous either way.

There must be something icy in my gaze,
because Ned now sports a wounded expression.
Justine puts a comforting hand on his forearm.
"Don't take out your frustration on Ned."

"I'm sorry." I stand up fast.

The Overton brochure flutters to the floor;
I say "Got it" before Ned can bend to retrieve it for me.
"Really. I didn't mean anything. Gonna head for band."

Now they're watching me as I set down my tray,
make for the door.

24

The bell hasn't rung.
I wish I could make myself keep walking
to the end of the hall,
out to the back bleachers
where I'm sure Dave is "catching rays."
He probably doesn't hold on to things
like memories of mis-tucked second-grade skirts.
He doesn't wave signs asking people
to vote him into a powerless Student Council office.

It feels like he lives, instead of always making plans—
the opposite of my eternally scheduled life
that offers so little pleasure in the now.
Maybe that's why I can be hot for Dave.
If he doesn't want to get to class on time,
doesn't want to go to college,
I bet he has his reasons.
Maybe he needs extra time to rumple his hair
so it looks that good.
Maybe he thinks deep thoughts
while he sits,

whittling sticks with a school-banned pocketknife,
stealing glances at the sky.

Dave makes me want things. Not good-girl things.
I've never done anything beyond kissing a boy,
but now I whisper under my breath,
"I wanna get under you, Dave Miller,"
and other phrases I've heard
on the HBO movies I watch at the end of the night
after Steven's in bed and my parents have retreated
to their Civil War bases:
Mom in the kitchen, Dad in his office.

"I want you."

"I need you."

"I burn for you."

I picture myself riding with Dave in his patchwork Fiesta,
stopping in a wooded spot,
without a time or plan to return to reality.
Sometimes the dream turns rough, dangerous,
As if we were mafia lovers by a New Jersey highway;
other times things are soft, gentle, PG-13,
in a meadow of flowers in saturated hues.

I am a good girl he rescued from embarrassment,
a bad girl wearing studded bracelets.

Everything I know about sex
I've learned from HBO.

25

Friday is the worst night of the week,
the beginning of the eternal weekend,
two whole days without school for Steven,
without yoga for Mom:
without a real excuse, like work, to set Dad free.

Around when Steven turned ten,
Dad added running, then golf,
to his hours of ever-increasing "ambition" at the office.

I don't like it, but I get it.

I think one reason I'm so good at trumpet,
practice so much,
is that it's always an unassailable argument
to escape from my family.

26

New Hampshire State Youth Orchestra
fills Saturday mornings. I confess,
my heart belongs more and more to jazz
(Dave Miller aside)
than classical,
but it's good practice, with pretty good musicians,
and Justine sometimes meets me for Thai food after.

"So, what did your parents say about Overton?" she asks
as we divide an order of chicken satay between us,
ask for extra peanut sauce.

"I didn't tell them."

"Daisy, they'd be thrilled Mr. Orson wants to
recommend you."

It's hard to explain the complexity of my worries,
even to Justine,
who loves my mother's cookies,
who still says she's willing to come over
and hang with me and Steven

when my folks aren't home
even though she's a little bit afraid,
even though I don't really ask her anymore.

"I think I want to surprise them.
You know, they could use some good news."

"But isn't there an application fee?"
Justine is always practical.

And this I do dare ask, because Justine has a credit card
and a mother who, guilty over her divorce,
hardly ever questions, while my parents,
though they usually give me what money I ask for
(since I hardly ever do),
always ask the what, where, why,
start conversations I don't always want to have.

"Do you think we could put it on your credit card?
I'd pay you back."
"Su-ure," Justine says.

I can see in her eyes she's not convinced,
knows there's more to this story.
I promise myself I'll explain the whole thing
soon.

As soon as I get accepted, tell my parents the truth.

Sooner, maybe.

27

Sunday is for trumpet practice—
as much as I can get
between spelling Mom for a trip to Safeway,
keeping watch on Steven
while Dad golfs and Mom cooks,
sitting at our kitchen table foursome for dinner
while Mom regales us with some complicated story
about looking for a venetian bronze planter
for the back patio
and the sales clerk repeatedly showing her pieces
made of brass.

Dad looks as miserable as Ned Hoffman in the wake of Dave Miller,
which makes me travel inside my head
to an HBO place where I imagine Dave and me
doing something they preface with
AC—Adult Content,
N—Nudity,
before running the opening credits.

And when I'm not thinking that,
the secret I am keeping from my parents
pulses in the front of my brain
until I worry the words "Application to Overton"
will burn through the inside of my skull,
the letters emerging like a charred tattoo across my brow.

"Delicious dinner, Mom."
I rush my half-eaten plate of roast chicken,
braised kale, to the sink,
resist the urge to cover my forehead with my hand.

28

"What are your musical inspirations?"

My fingers hover over the school library media center
keyboard as I search my mind for the words
to answer my first Overton application question.
If they mean what makes me keep on playing,
the answer is too complicated for words on paper.
It's not just the compositions I've learned and played
and heard.
It's not just so I can be an easy source of pride
for my parents.
It's not just because a tiny part of me still believes
Mom's long-abandoned pile
of medical journal clippings
about music freeing the autistic mind.
It's not even just that I can't imagine stopping
because I know, like Miles Davis
halfway through *Kind of Blue*,
that I haven't reached the end, an end . . .

If they mean why I'm writing this application,
it's because I need to know that, someday,

I might be able to escape from my house.
I need to do something besides practice and help, cower
and wait.

Summer is far away,
but I think I can survive at home that long.
Then I need to get into Overton. Or go *somewhere.*
Can I write that?

I open another window on the computer,
search for "summer teen music programs."
There's one in California that I recognize,
several at colleges here in New England.
Some look too expensive; others have application fees
I'll find a way to manage.
I start a list with Overton at the top.
Then six more places.

Enough.
I close the search window,
refocus my mind on the essay.
Mom has yoga tonight,
and I can only stay a few more minutes.
There'd be little risk of my parents catching me writing
the application essays at home.

They're so busy taking care of Steven
and avoiding being in charge of Steven
and holding on to some kind of life around Steven
that sometimes it feels they've half forgotten
I'm even living there.
Still, I feel safer doing it here at school.

"Musical inspirations, huh?"
Dave's hand rests casually on my shoulder as he reads the screen.

I shiver at his touch,
thrilled yet instantly on guard
against my summer plans
becoming part of the unspoken yet known lore of Jasper,
picturing Andy Bouchard offhandedly asking Dad,
"Has Daisy heard from Overton yet?"
as he hands him a cup of strong, black French roast.
I stand up, turn to block Dave's view of the monitor.
"Don't see much of you in the library."

"Then you haven't been looking hard enough,
Daisy-brains.
I come by most Monday afternoons at some point.
Like to read in that chair."
Dave points to the egg-shaped, plastic-and-pleather

chair that forms a weird centerpiece
between rows of fiction.

I often steal the occasional half hour in the library
on Monday afternoons.
Wouldn't I have remembered
seeing Dave lounging in egg leather?
I look at my watch. It's almost five o'clock.

"Shit! I'm gonna be late for—
It's my mom's yoga night and—"

I save the document onto my flash drive, shut down,
cram the application, list, textbooks,
papers into my backpack.
Run for the parking lot.

29

"Where were you?
I texted four times!"
Mom accuses, before adding,
"I was worried."

"I was in the library studying.
I lost track of the time.
Just go to yoga now. It's fine."

But Steven has noticed Mom's frantic, angry tone;
picked up something about the sweat on my upper lip,
my rushed footsteps.
His hands start to twist, eyes roll upward,
searching or maybe seeing nothing.

"Look what you've done," Mom says.
She turns to my brother. "Steven. Steven, are you okay?"

She knows better than to reach for him, touch him.
Together we watch.
"Want a cookie, Steven? Chocolate chip," I try.

But he flinches at the burping whoosh
that opens the stay-fresh cookie bin.

"Damn. I haven't taken him to the bathroom yet,"
Mom murmurs.

"Come on, Steven, let's go watch Batman."
I stupidly try to take his hand,
but he yanks it away, twisting his palms together.
With a wail, the pacing begins, slow and awkward,
around the edges of the kitchen.
He smacks his head against the doorframe.

Mom and I are frozen statues watching a tornado:
transfixed, terrified, unable to take cover.

"I'm calling your father.
Did we forget your meds this morning, Steven?"
she asks in her calming voice as she moves slowly
toward the phone,
trying to help him connect with some idea, some word,
some safe, ritual notion
that will halt the danger, reconnect him to our world.
She pauses, holding the receiver as if it might sting her.
"I haven't had to interrupt him at work in weeks."

"Don't!" I cry out.
Then, "Don't," more softly, smiling at Steven
even though I know he isn't seeing me.
"I have an idea."

I pull out my trumpet case,
searching my mind for something soft, simple . . .
I attach the mouthpiece,
press the valves a few times,
take a breath.

I try a few measures of the andante section of
Hummel's *Trumpet Concerto*
I've pulled from my music folder.
By the second page, his hands slow their writhing.
Mom, still as stone, just watches
as I try to play with the least possible motion—
no grandstanding,
no dipping my horn up and down like I'm in a marching band.
Soft, steady, twice as slow
as the Youth Orchestra conductor would've wanted it,
slower still as Steven finally stops, and mumbles
something that Mom hears as, "Cookie?"
She hands him two,
which she'd let him eat right there on the kitchen floor,

but Steven moves like a robot to his seat at the table, waits
until she brings him a napkin and a plate.

Soon crumbs litter the floor.

"What would I do without you?"
Mom says as she moves for the dustpan and broom.

"I'm so sorry you missed yoga, Mom."

30

"I'm sorry?" I whisper
the question to myself
as I creep down the stairs with my trumpet.

"Sorry," I say aloud
as I shut the door of my basement practice room.

It's a word I say every time I feel like I'm the cause
of an outburst by Steven,
every time I get a grade lower than an A-minus,
or do something else to disrupt the equilibrium of our lives.

"Sorry!" I shout.
I've said it so many times
it has dissolved from syllables to sounds,
like those times when you look at yourself in the mirror
and see skin and teeth and hair
more than a face.

I close my mouth, look around
at my parents' great investment

in their musical daughter:
a padded cell,
in voguish colors, of course.

Mom tried.
There's a high-end synthesizer in one corner,
a bust of Haydn beside a vase of dried flowers,
a vintage varnished wood music stand,
and two cozy "listening chairs,"
their upholstery fabric strewn with black quarter notes,
the kind of custom material for which my mother trolls the Internet.
Though she hardly ever comes down to hear me play anymore,
and never with Dad.

Safe in my soundproof tomb,
I can close my mind to the absurdity upstairs.
Pedal tones and long tones fill half an hour of practice.
Now the time is 6:12
and my quirky mind notes that twelve is six times two.

I've spent too many nights
watching the LED lights on my alarm clock,
waiting for 11:10 to turn to 11:11—one, one, one, one;
too many days

hearing about my “uncanny,” “unchildlike”
dedication to practicing trumpet,
copiously copying symbols and colors
onto the white canvas of so many pairs of sneakers,
reading books recommended by Mom,
support groups, well-meaning outsiders,
meant to reassure me of the beauties, the gifts of living
with a special-needs sibling,
not to arrive at the question:

Is there something autistic about me, too?

There is research
backing a genetic component to the disability,
and some likelihood of autism running in families.

More evidence is that horrible sense of distance
I cannot close
between me and my best friend;
the way I cannot sort my feelings for Dave,
the desire from the fear;
how I want to smack my palms and bang my head
until it all goes away,
like I've watched my brother do
too many times to count.

The thoughts tsunami through my mind,
powerful waves of terror.
My heart begs me to silence my brain.
My embouchure rested, I retreat to beats and measures,
resume the glorious, focused effort of practicing.
For more than an hour, I work at slurs and songs.
My lips buzz into numbness.
I should take a break,
but I push through another series of pedal tones,
low strengthening notes,
before I set down the trumpet,
drop breathless into the nearest "listening chair."

Whisper again,
"I'm sorry."

31

"Daisy?" Mr. Orson catches me
as I'm assembling my trumpet
before the start of jazz band.
"I wanted to talk to you about the holiday concert.
I'd like you to play a solo. Something festive.
I've got some pieces for you to try out.
Pick something you like. Maybe talk it over with Aggie."

"Um, okay." I take the folder of sheet music
from his hand. Add the task
of bringing the pages with me to my next lesson
with my private trumpet teacher, Aggie Nedrum,
to my epic to-do list.

Why don't I open my mouth, say "I just don't have time
to learn another song
between practice, schoolwork, and my brother"?
But I can't,
or won't.
I just enjoy Mr. Orson's approving smile
as a jaw-snapping yawn splits my face.

And the emotion I feel isn't sorrow but anger
at being imprisoned in an autism family.

We start in on the Ellington piece,
a smooth swing number called "Almost Cried."
I spit each angry thought into the notes I play,
getting louder, fiercer, than I ever can in my own home,
well, any part of it except the basement.

"Daisy, a little gentler, please. You're getting off tempo,"
Mr. Orson says in that kindly, unaccusing way he has,
which, today, makes me burst into tears
while the ten jazz guys (including Cal) stare
and the three other girls mouth "on her period"
to each other.

"Excuse me, Mr. O."
I set my horn as roughly as I dare on my chair,
dash out the door,
turn toward the girls' bathroom,
but find myself rushing headlong
into the "Yes I Didn't!" T-shirted chest of Dave Miller.

"Hey there, Daisy-brains."
Do I feel him pull me toward him for a second
before taking my shoulders and putting me straight?

"You okay?"

"Yeah!" I say, adding intense mortification on a dozen
levels to my misery.
Mumble as I twist out of his grasp,
"Yeah, I'm just terrific."

I make it to the bathroom
without crashing into anyone else.
Blessedly, it is empty and I can let go my shuddering sobs
without locking myself in a stall
and hoping no one recognizes my ink-covered Keds.

By the time the homeroom bell rings, it is over.
I splash my face with water,
rub away the mascara streaks as best I can.
Before I leave the bathroom, I text Mom.
"After-school project meeting. Home by seven."

I have no idea what I'll do between last period and seven
at night,
but I won't do it in the prison.

32

In A-PUSH, the words Mr. Angelli scrawls
on the whiteboard blur before my weep-worn eyes.
My head droops against the window;
the foreboding chill of near winter
seeps from the glass pane into my scalp.
Phrases filter aimlessly into my resistant ears.

In the Emancipation Proclamation,
Abraham Lincoln declares that
"all persons held as slaves . . .
henceforward shall be free."

If a slave is someone
who cannot make her own choices,
whose life is scheduled, controlled,
then aren't I a slave?
Don't I deserve emancipation
from Mom and Dad, who schedule my actions?
From Steven, whose whims rule my spirits?

Where are the "liberty and justice" for me in life's equation?

33

I can feel Justine's worried eyes boring into the back of my skull
as I take down history notes with weary deliberation,
go through the motions
of free will.

"Tomorrow, we'll take a partial practice AP test,"
Mr. Angelli announces, as if that's some kind of fun.
He closes his notebook.
We all follow suit, me rather loudly.

"Hey there." I look up to see Cal-for-short
hovering over my desk.

"If you need tutoring, ask Justine," I sigh.

"Uh, no. Just wanted to be sure you were okay there, after . . ."
A faint pinkness
travels up the back of Cal's neck to his ears.

"After what?" Justine pipes in behind us.

"Daisy here . . . she, well . . .
she had a rough band practice this mornin'."
Now his face is a full-blown blush,
redder than Justine's when she gets angry.

"You can tell her I cried."
I stand up and grab my books to my chest.

"I just didn't think I should . . . I mean . . .
It wasn't mine to tell."

Justine looks worried, puts her arm around my shoulders,
guides me toward the door.
There is no place where I can go to rest, to be free,
so I just let her lead me down the hall.

"What were you crying for, Daisy?"
she asks when we're outside the French classroom.

"I think my parents might be getting a divorce,"
is what I say, though where the thought came from
is as mysterious
as the question of who truly masterminded
the plot to kill Lincoln.

34

Divorces are all different.
Dave's parents' was the kind of fiasco
that turns one happy-ish upper-middle-class family
into two less happy, poorer ones.
Justine's family's was a quiet dissolution
in which she and Shirley, her mom,
stayed in the same house,
repainted thoroughly in lavenders, pinks,
erasing all traces of the man
who had tired of lawns, encumbrances, women,
and simply walked into the sunset, into another life,
leaving a giant chunk of change
and a mountainous lump of bitter disbelief
behind him.

Now that the word *divorce* has escaped my lips,
tied itself to my family, my fears,
Justine is glued to my side.
After school, we hang out in the student commons
until four o'clock,
when she has to leave for her voice lesson.

"You sure you'll be okay?" she asks as we stand at our side-by-side lockers.

"Yeah. I'll be fine," I answer.

It might be true.
If divorce happened, would things change for the better?
Would I be able to practice music someplace other than the basement sometimes?

Alone by my locker, I whisper to myself,
"My parents may be getting a divorce,"
draw the *c* out into a long hiss,
find a kind of softness in the word.
Part of me wishes it would happen,
that my parents would shatter something
beyond the toys and dishes Steven breaks.
Maybe it would make me stronger
like Justine, like Dave;
braver, more independent.

I wander up the hall to the library,
determined to fill the hours from now till seven,
to make a point by my absence from home,
as if Mom will ever see me

as a laborer on strike, a slave in rebellion.

I will finish the Overton application today.
For my musical inspiration,
I'll write about Miles Davis,
about *Kind of Blue*.

I put buds in my ears,
call the tune up on my phone,
and feel that album fill and float my heart
the way it always does.

The egg chair is empty.
With time to burn, I decide on half an hour of listening
before I start my essay,
but ensconced in the black leather,
science-fiction-style seat,
I fall asleep.

"Hey, you're in my chair."
A boot is kicking my Keds.
It's dark inside my egg cocoon, and it takes a few minutes
to go from unconscious to vaguely conscious to
"Who in the—?"

"Tired much?" Dave asks, ignoring my hostile greeting.

He smiles his tantalizing smile
into the oval entrance of the egg.

I yank the buds from my ears.
"This chair is damned comfy."

"Don't I know it. Move over."

Without waiting for me to speak or slide,
Dave drops into the chair beside me,
shoving until there's enough room for us both to be
half-comfortable,
which suddenly becomes awesomely cozy as DAVE
OMG-I-wish-Justine-were-here-to-see-this MILLER
slides his arm over my shoulders and draws me close.

"You okay? Seemed like you were having a shit morning."
His voice is low. His breath tickles my ear.

"I'm okay." I let my head loll against his shoulder,
close my eyes, wonder at how a morning of sobs
can morph into my own unbelievable,
real-life HBO movie moment.

35

I hear the second hand of my old-school Swatch watch
tick-tick-tick around its giant plastic dial.
Dave leans back, closes his eyes,
and just sits with me.
I try to stop the million thoughts—
fantasy, fear, what-is-happening-here,
wish-I-could-tell-someone,
I-should-be-writing-the-Overton-application—
racing through my brain
and let myself be silent
like Dave.

36

A few minutes before six,
the librarian starts her gentle tour,
quietly letting the few remaining students in the study
carrels, around the stacks,
know that it's time to close up.
Her eyes open a little wider
when she gets to the egg chair,
but she just taps our two pairs of knees and says,
"Time to go."

Embarrassed, I leap up,
almost smack my head on the upper lip of the egg.
Dave is slower, unashamed.
"Wanna grab a bite somewhere?" he asks.

"Somewhere quick, I guess. I've gotta be home by seven."

"I'll drive you."

"But my car is in the parking lot."

"I'll bring you back here then," he says.

I nod, follow him to his vintage (well, late nineties)
Ford Fiesta in the corner of the parking lot.

"You've got a gorgeous mouth, Daisy-brains."
He pushes me with gentle roughness
against the car door.
I know what's coming, close my eyes,
but still I gasp when his lips hit mine,
a little hard, a little hungry,
nothing like the tentative kisses I've traded
with boys from youth orchestra,
Or the silly, innocent pecks exchanged
In the semi-public of summer night bonfire parties by
the lake.

His hands don't go to my shoulders, my hair.
Instead his left arm encircles my ribs,
just under my arms;
he draws me in, kissing so powerfully my head bounces
against the driver's side window.
I feel his tongue pushing my lips apart . . .

HBO warnings start flashing in my mind:
A blurry AC—adult content—

and the threat of encroaching N—nudity—
blink in sleek yellow letters
against the gray-black screen of my eyelid interiors.
I squirm out from under his fierce embrace.

"I should get going. I'm . . . I'm not hungry."
I don't look back as I trot across the lot to my beige Subaru.

37

I try to ignore Dave's car,
right behind mine as I turn onto Main;
try not to look at his half-amused,
half-annoyed expression haunting my rearview mirror.
I feel a whoosh of relief when he goes left at Broad Street
and I keep going straight.

A ring around my ribs still vibrates
with the memory-sensation of Dave Miller's grasp.
My mind fills with wonder, yearning
for whatever might have happened next,
yet I can't understand—
beyond our baby-days romance,
why would Dave Miller be drawn to me,
the trumpet girl?
Maybe it's all those jokes about buzzing lips
and what that power might be good for
inside a boy's jeans.

I know that sometimes there's a bit of bragging
where my classmates tell their friends how our high school
has the All-State number one brass player,

how I've won competitions
from New England down to Florida.
I'm a feather in their cap
even if my lips never move south of there.
Stupid jokes—being a trumpet girl, I've heard 'em all.
But somewhere in there, is there the why,
the logic that could connect the dots
between Dave Miller and me?

38

Despite my plan, I get home before seven.
Rebellion failed.
Steven is staring toward some cartoon
on the little kitchen television
while Mom loads the dishwasher.

"There's a plate for you in the fridge, Daisy."

"Hey, hon." Dad surprises me
by coming through the door.
"Shower time, Steven!"
he says with enormous fake cheer,
doesn't bother to smile.
Steven doesn't seem to respond to Dad's expressions,
so there is no point in looking any happier,
unhappier, than he feels,
and Dad is pretty much always far beyond blue.

The plate is a giant chef salad
that looks delicious,
especially because it's been more than twelve hours

since anything but cafeteria food landed in my stomach.
I sit alone at the kitchen island,
watch Mom's furious arms scrub pots and pans in the sink.
Her hair is up in a ponytail,
the knobby bones of her spine a ladder of anxiety.

I cram my mouth until
the awful, flat wailing begins floating down the stairs,
accompanied by Dad's attempts at not shouting,
which fail:
"Steven, Steven, close your eyes or they'll get full of soap.
Steven, this is just water.
Steven, hang on, Steven.
Shit!"
Growing ever tenser, less mock-cheerful.

Mom leans her weight against the counter's edge,
hands framing the sink, elbows bent.
I watch her try to yoga-breathe,
count, prepare to go upstairs
and mop the sloshed and soapy battleground
Dad will have abandoned
as soon as Steven is passably clean.

"Gonna go start practicing." I set my half-full plate
on the counter.

She doesn't mention the waste
or ask for explanation.
We all know.

39

I stare at my horn, freed from its case,
as if it were half a stranger,
not a comfortable extension of my arm, my voice.

Three simple valves
I have pressed nearly every day for eight years,
buzzing, tonguing, even singing into the mouthpiece,
sometimes feeling like it's the only way I can free
the secrets of my heart.

But tonight, in this tasteful basement,
I worry that my forward momentum has stalled.
Perhaps I will even, like Steven, regress.

I know my brother has lost more—
never had so many of the things I have—
yet sometimes it's hard not to blame him for my descent
from orchestra-guest-artist-worthy
prodigy horn player at ten or eleven
to mere highly capable teen trumpeter, winner of things
like ribbons and high school plaudits.

Maybe that's all I am now.

Are my parents the devils
who shot me from highest grace?
Or are they simply the arrows fired by Steven,
who has morphed from challenging autistic boy
to dangerous, nonverbal near-man?
Are they, like me,
victims of genetics and circumstance,
targets and weapons in a war
that is happening inside my brother's mind?
Either way, they pierce me with their flagging energy,
decreasing allotments of time
to come with me to master classes,
regional competitions,
to hear me perform.

Is seventeen old enough
to not need a mother and father anymore?
Should I not care
that Dad doesn't tuck me into bed at night,
nor mind that there's no time
to confide in Mom that Dave asked me to the movies?
Is this the way it ought to be?
All I know for certain is that
here I am

without showers of attention;
with fewer trips, fewer prizes,
hour after hour
trying to make a sound like Miles Davis,
imagining jazz as a cure
for the blues.

40

Ten o'clock
should be quiet.

Ten o'clock,
the warriors should be back at their separate bases.

Instead,
Mom and Dad have closed the pocket doors,
sealed themselves inside the kitchen.
And I hear whispering, the occasional loud word.

I retreat to the solace of the family room television,
but HBO provides no relief.
The naked, writhing bodies of the historical miniseries
remind me only of Dave Miller, what I wanted,
what I feared.
I study the girls' breasts, some huge and pendulous,
some small and firm;
consider my own, somewhere in between, I think.
Enough for Dave Miller, I guess.
Consider my face, pretty enough,

though maybe not for television,
the nose a little buttonish,
the mouth a little wide.

Now there is a Roman king, speaking of power
to a woman who tries to wield her own
through the translucent gauze of her dress.
(I love the British accents, which make even seduction
seem like art.)

I wish
that my parents still shared a bed,
that Dad did not sleep in the extra room beside Steven's
while Mom has the master to herself.

On television, a kiss,
a slap.
No resolution.

I pull out my phone.
Text Justine:

"Did your parents start talking more
right before the divorce?"

But she doesn't reply.

Real time has passed.
It's now almost eleven.
Maybe she's asleep.

Eleven,
and Steven is quiet.
The credits are running,
HBO tantalizing viewers with promises
of more passion next Tuesday night.

Just past eleven,
the pocket doors to the kitchen still drawn,
the whispering goes on.
No answers.

41

Wednesday's breakfast,
dutiful as usual, yet there's something less resistant
about the weight of Dad's tread
on the kitchen hardwood,
which yields, instead of comfort,
a sense of impending doom.

The *dah-nah-nah-nah-nah* of *Phantom of the Opera.*
The *dee-up, dee-up, dee-up*
of John Williams's *Jaws* movie score
as the shark's narrow fin emerges, razorlike,
from the ocean's surface.

The threat throbbing
through the silence of Dad's absent criticism
as Mom stoops belatedly
to tie my brother's shoes.

42

I am so embroiled in my family horror story
I don't think to tell Justine about Dave Miller
and the egg chair and the parking lot
until we're in the girls' room after lunch.
Her squeal is so glass-shatteringly loud it draws my eye
to the bathroom mirror
in search of cracks.

"And you didn't text me *that* last night?"
She gives me a soft pinch.

"There was a lot going on. My parents . . ."

"Oh, but no,
my parents didn't talk more before the divorce.
Maybe they're trying to make up," she suggests.
"But, back to Dave," she says. "How *was* it?"

Two other girls come through the bathroom door.
We exchange polite hi-but-you-can't-hear-my-secrets
glances.

Justine puts her lipstick back in her purse,
drags me into the hall.

"Let's go find him!" she says.
"He's usually out on the bleachers
behind the school after lunch, right?"

I don't know how to explain the power of his kiss,
something hard to understand.
Not as terrifying as the force in Steven's arm
when he smashes a dish.
Yet, with both, I never quite know
if it's entirely innocent, if it can be at all controlled.
What is it
when someone so close to you
makes you hurt, a lot or a little,
in action or in circumstance?

"It kind of didn't end well," I tell Justine.
"Besides, I want to do some work on my Overton
application."

"More good news for your parents!" she declares.

"Yeah," I say.

But all I know for certain
is that despite the calm of the morning,
Dad still didn't kiss Mom good-bye.

43

"Describe some of the ensembles in which you play"
is the prompt for the second essay
of the Overton application I am frantic to finish.
If my parents split up, will going away to music camp be harder or easier?
Will Steven be less my responsibility
or more?

The worries clutter my straight-A mind,
which has gotten me through all kinds of essays,
from a sunny "My Summer Vacation"
to the endlessly boring *Moby-Dick*.

This should not be so hard. I try to calm myself.
This should be about jazz versus classical,
band versus orchestra versus playing in the basement alone.

Yet, when I hit "save" on the keyboard,
I have managed just three lines:

Playing a solo is very different from being in an ensemble.
Even if your own standard of perfection is constant,
different mistakes are more noticeable,
different skills are more valuable in different groups.

And I'm off,
with my unfinished essays and all my other burdens,
to figure out how to say,
"We had gone to the beach,"
"He had arrived at the beach,"
"They had wanted to go to the beach,"
en français.

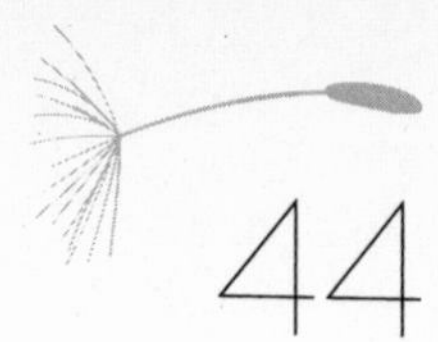

44

Yoga
is bullshit to me
but salvation for my mother.
I do not see how "downward dog" and "tree"
can bring her some kind of peace. I think
it is the music of the voices around her;
the quiet lull of the instructor's voice, encouraging;
the birdlike chatter of the other moms, who,
after bending and stretching, cluster round her, listen
to the tune she plays, the horrible, discordant song
of Dad and me,
of Steven,
of inescapable tension, of worry,
of hoping today won't be as bad as yesterday,
that tomorrow won't be worse.
That is yoga for my mother,
while I sit and wait
for Dad to oblige us all by coming home
before Steven hits me
out of some incomprehensible frustration
or tosses something hard against a wall.

Why do we pretend
that there is any kind of harmony in our house?
Thank God there is music at school,
at band,
at orchestra.
Thank God there are places
with sounds that make me cry
from beauty,
not from pain.

45

"C'mon, Steven, bedtime,"
Dad says as he comes through the door,
drops his briefcase by the hall table.

No hello, no "how was your day?"
Even if Steven's reactions are often nonexistent,
it seems to me inhumane to behave that way.
No wonder Mom twitches at the sight
of Dad and Steven together.

I think Dad loves him in some way.

I remember when I was small, before I realized
that Steven wasn't like other little brothers,
that his staring and stimming were not games
for me to imitate;
when I thought we lived a normal life,
when my parents both assured me
that, despite everything, we could.
A tiny ball of this emotion still curls deep inside me,
still stirs when I remember

pushing cars along the edges
of the family room carpet beside Steven
and smiling at him
and not thinking much of anything
about his failure to smile back.
I want to believe
there's a place like that inside my father's heart, too.

As Dad slides a hand under his arm,
gets ready to encourage him up off the couch,
I try to look into Steven's eyes:
matching brother-and-sister blue with mine
but different in every other aspect.

Steven does not meet my gaze, and yet
when I play for him, there's something I know,
some connection
that stretches past the neurological limits,
the things the doctors tell us he can know,
can feel,
can express.

There is something
there
inside,
kind of magical,
kind of unique.

"Up we go," Dad says.
Together they move slowly to the door,
Steven beginning to wring his hands, knowing—
without us ever learning how—
that the time has come
for bathroom, bed, things he does not enjoy.
"Easy does it, big boy."

Despite Dad's tension, I remember
just days ago
one of Steven's explosions yielded
to a melody.

Despite the new forearm bruise
Mom's short-sleeved yoga shirt cannot hide,
despite the whirling, flailing bombs
that explode with barely a warning,
despite the resistance to everything not routine,
to everything wet and cold,
to everything spicy, loud,
I still want to believe
there is

something kind of
kind.

46

The second Dad and Steven head for the stairs,
the evil ritual of pajamas,
brushing teeth with bubble gum toothpaste,
tepid water,
I run, not to the quiet of the basement
but up to my bedroom
to write the rest of the Overton application.
The words of the essays fly from my fingertips
fast as musical scales.

Breathlessly, I complete another application,
and another,
casting desperate lines out into a lake of alternatives:
to Philadelphia, Los Angeles, Boston, Maine . . .
I open the tin box on the top of my desk,
count out the eighty-two dollars inside it.
I can probably get Mom to write one application check
for the Boston school,
since it's not too expensive, nor too far away.
I can pretend all the kids in jazz band are applying to it,
like an assignment.

Justine will cover what fees I can't manage
until I can pay her back.

Cut and paste, search and replace:
My "musical inspirations" and "performance histories"
are tweaked for each program.
I want to have it all typed and saved
so it can be sent out
and I won't have to think anymore, to wonder
if I'll dare.

It's late when I finish,
but I need to practice,
even if it's just for half an hour.
So I turn off my computer,
tiptoe down to the basement.

47

Passing the kitchen, I pause at the pocket doors,
slid shut again.
Hear voices rise and fall. Tones sharpen and mellow.

I think of the stories Mom and Dad used to tell
about meeting in a college history class.
(Romance and A-PUSH? Unimaginable.)
About getting together for an after-class beer one night
and talking on and on
about the role of folk music in cultural transitions.
(Yes, they were both super-nerds.)
About singing together.
(I get my musical talent from somewhere.)

Could something behind that door be mended
with a song? Should I remind them
of their mutual love of history, of music?
Would they try harder if they knew how badly
I want them to fix what's broken in this house
beyond the kicked-in closets and shattered dishes?

Or is what's here unfixable,
like Steven, simply beyond repair?

"I need a shower." Mom is using her exasperated tone.

"I've got e-mails to write."
Dad's voice is nearly emotionless, flat,
defeated.

48

"I finished the applications!" I announce to Justine
in homeroom that morning.

"Let's go to my house after school
and submit everything," Justine says.
Her excited grin is infectious, her voice so loud
Ashleigh Anderson sneers in our direction.

It's Thursday, so no yoga.
I text Mom the plan, get the okay.

Justine is unlocking her front door by 3:15.
Her mother is still at work, as usual.
She refills the dog's water dish, pours us two Cokes
while I scratch Dickens behind his soft cocker spaniel ears.

Up in Justine's pink room,
we log on to the Overton website.
I cut and paste my essays into the appropriate boxes.
She types in the credit card name, address, number.

We clink soda glasses and click "send."
I e-mail Mr. Orson the instructions for sending his
recommendation.

"Woo-hoo!" Justine cheers.

"Now the Danielson Conservatory Program," I say.
"That's the one in upstate New York."

An hour later, we flop onto her rose chenille bedspread.

"I can't believe I did it," I say.

"Your parents are going to be *so* surprised when you get into all these programs."

"If I get in," I correct her,
though Justine and I both know my chances are good.

"I bet it'll be Overton," she says.
"Imagine, a summer in sunny Pennsylvania."

"Is it sunny?"

"I don't know. It'll feel sunny to you, I bet.

All that music.
All that peace."

I wonder how wrong it was not to tell my parents,
to borrow application money, to be so secretive.

"Wanna stay for supper?" Justine offers.
"Mom could bring home pizza."

"I can't," I say,
because my mother has already texted
that she wants me home.
I guess she needs a break.

49

But it's not a break Mom needs.
At least, she is not alone.
Dad is sitting at the kitchen table,
watching Steven chew methodically through a cookie.

There's no smell of dinner in the air,
no moist green aroma of steaming broccoli
or warm welcome of something roasting.
No "Kiss the Cook" apron covers
Mom's T-shirt and jeans.

"Glad you're home, Daisy." Dad smiles.

"We've ordered Chinese," Mom says.

"But Steven doesn't like . . ." I feel my voice trail away,
watching my brother's innocence while my heart
has, possibly literally, stopped in my chest. I wait,
ears throbbing with heat, for the
"sit down, we've got something to tell you,"
for the "your Mom and I have tried, but this marriage . . ."

Do I take my usual solitary spot at the kitchen island?
Sit willingly at the table like a lamb at the slaughter?
I feel all limbs and fire,
suddenly furiously angry at Steven.

How can he sit there?
How can this—*this*—
not trigger the rocking, the smashing,
the need to call Dad at work?

Bite, bite, bite. Warm cookie in mouth.
Swallows of milk to wash down the sweetness.
Crumbs scattering like garden seeds
on the barren hardwood floor.

"Holy shit, what is going on?"
I slap my hand on the granite countertop.
"Just. Tell. Me!"

And I, of course, succeed where they failed.
With a wail
Steven stands up, grabs his chair,
and shoves it to the floor.

Even after I whisper "sorry," bow my head,
his violent momentum cannot be stopped.

It's a bad one, long-lasting.
Luckily Dad is here with his strong arms
to protect Mom and me
while he looks over Steven's thrown-back head,
mouths "see what I mean" to Mom.

The doorbell sounds with the long, intense rings
of someone who has tried several times without success.
It's the Chinese food delivery guy,
wearing an exasperated expression.
Mom apologizes, pays cash with a giant tip.

We leave the neatly knotted, steaming white plastic bags
on the counter
untouched for two hours.

Afterward, Steven locked into his bedroom,
pocket doors open,
Mom and Dad invite me inside.
Over plates of congealed cashew chicken, cold rice,
they talk a long riff about autism, adolescence,
family dynamics, marriage,
skidding and turning while I wait for the word—
divorce—
that never comes.

Instead:
"Your Mom and I have decided"—
Dad looks over my head at my mother,
who is trembling a little,
her eyes, slightly wet, gazing
at some spot on the far kitchen wall—
"that it would be better for Steven,
for all of us,
if he were moved to a group home,
a sort of boarding school for kids like him,
where they could support his needs, keep him safe,
maybe teach him some skills for the future,
like tying his own shoes."

He stops.
The house grows so impossibly still
I can feel the air quiver,
the earth rotate beneath our feet.
Or maybe it's the oxygen rushing from my lungs,
the blood from my head.
I am going to fall down.
I cannot balance on this planet
twisting in an altered universe.

What?

Where?

Questions stagger into my brain,
but I cannot push them through my lips.

"It's not going to happen right away."
Mom's voice is as unsteady as my heart.
"There's more to do, paperwork and visits and things."

I nod, not sure if I am understanding her words,
unable to process this digression
from the divorce I had anticipated.
Instead . . .
This is the unthinkable.

"This wasn't an easy choice, Daisy.
There are a lot of factors," Dad says.

"Your father put Steven on a couple
of program wait-lists last summer."
The tendons in Mom's neck stand out
like barren winter trees.
Her tone is both accusing and grateful.
"We didn't think we'd need . . ."

Dad's voice is low and deliberate.

"The program director feels that Steven
is no longer a fit for the special-needs classroom.
Mom can't handle him here, all day, every day, alone.
We could try hiring more home health aids,
people like that,
but what if he hurts someone besides himself—
a repairman or caregiver?
That would wreak havoc on our lives, our finances,
our futures.
Your future."

His eyes follow me the same way they watch Steven
when Dad thinks he's about to erupt.

But I am the good-girl ghost
who floats past the dining table to the kitchen island,
disappears before Dad's out the door,
quietly watches Steven line Blokus tiles end to end.

"I'm gonna go downstairs and practice,"
is the sentence I manage to force
through my clenched throat,
feeling nearly as wordless as Steven,
but I will not slap my own skull, my own mother.
I just need to go somewhere I can make a sound

that might burst through the horrible calm,
destroy the otherworldly stillness of this night.

50

I am numb as I leaf through my piles of sheet music.
There is the folder from Mr. Orson
with its cheery collection of holiday concert solos.
Unable to decide what to play,
I start with the top selection: "Silent Night."
The tune is easy and showcases my skill at high notes,
but the unsung lyrics mock me
with their tantalizing promise of heavenly peace.
I crumple the pages, shove them aside,
page angrily through the rest of the choices,
every one too hopeful.

I, the follower—
of scores, of schedules, of plans—
do not want to play these tunes.

I imagine my life as a collection of dates
for performances, competitions, lessons, tests.
Each high mark, prize, night of applause
leads to another,
another—

ambling eternally, destination unclear.
I cannot picture how this existence will look
when it is not counterpointed
by a different set of endless rituals
performed by my brother,
nor guided by my carefully honed formula
of words and actions
to protect my stoic parents,
conceal (as much as one can in Jasper)
the truth of how difficult home life has become.

How will I reply now when Justine asks me to sleep over?
Or if Dave ever invites me again to The Movie House?
How will I play a hopeful tune
or answer if, some quiet day down the road,
Mom, Dad, and I sit—
three at the breakfast table—
and they ask if I am happy?

Because as much as I am their good, steady daughter,
Steven is still my brother,
their son.

51

In the morning,
it feels like nothing has changed as I sit at the island
choking down rapidly softening Special K
while Steven eats his nine waffle bites row by row.
Mom chatters doggedly about whether to order
poinsettias from the local Scout troupe.
Dad ogles the paper as if the headline announces
the meaning of life.

Tink, tink: my spoon against the bright blue bowl.
Slurp: Steven gulping down his juice.
Something about a new pink-and-red flower variety
that holds its petals longer.

A chair pushed back.
Dad's "where the hell is his coat?"
And I wonder how it can be Friday,
this day that should have a new name:
the day after my parents announced
they are severing our family,

cutting off the mangled limb,
the one that made outsiders stare and the rest of us
limp along.
Twelve hours after they threw up their hands,
pushed my brother from a *Titanic* lifeboat
to save themselves—their marriage.
The first sun rising upon their assurances
that now I can live like an "ordinary" teenager.

I walk my cereal bowl to the sink.
Back turned, I let the word *ordinary* roll over my tongue,
longer, more staccato than *divorce*.
Ordinary:
a state to which I've never aspired in my *Kind of Blue* life;
a word that stung the few times it was ever tied
to me or my horn.
I hate them for offering it up as some kind of prize
when it feels more like an accusation;
that this decision they have made is partly my fault—
attributed to some unspoken desire of mine
to be less than exceptional.

"We're going to be late, Alice."
Dad's eyes are on his watch.

"I'm looking, Ted,"
Mom says softly but through clenched teeth,
pulling sweaters and fleeces
from the pegs by the back door,
searching for Steven's smooth nylon coat.

I am tempted by the vision of a morning
where she snaps back at my father,
"Look for it yourself!" in a strong voice;
of a home where anger can be set free, like love,
where I can sing aloud
to the song playing in my earbuds,
linger in the kitchen while Mom and Dad argue,
make up, stand close,
the way I remember them doing before Steven
got so big, so strong.

The thought dissolves as I watch Mom
push a wisp of hair off her brow,
gentle my brother into his jacket,
while Dad's foot taps as if he has somewhere urgent
to be, as if he cannot be delayed,
even for the briefest, coat-zipping space of time.

52

Before seven thirty, I am playing a jazz rendition of
"Adeste Fideles"—
"O Come, All Ye Faithful"—
a song of joining together,
of celebrating the birth of a savior.

I remember baby Steven
coming home from the hospital,
the house growing strangely dim,
voices whispering beyond Mom's tears.
When she'd been pregnant, Mom and I had read books
about caring for a new baby,
talked about how I could help with baths and bottles
and bringing toys.
But when Steven did arrive
no one let me hold him on my lap, give him a bottle.
Two years after the cord prolapse,
the emergency measures surrounding his birth
(though the doctors have told us we can never
truly know cause and effect),
the autism diagnosis became official,

though Mom, I think, always knew
what Steven's over-open, unfocused infant eyes,
the incessant way he toddler-drove red plastic cars
along the edges of carpets,
the sounds he didn't make,
were leading us toward.

"O come, let us adore Him!"

my trumpet declares,
while my heart falls, as it always does
when I wonder at the way the life we expected to have,
the family circle Steven was supposed to complete,
got somehow smudged, misdrawn; could never be
perfect, harmonic,
closed.

Were we cheated?

November is going to tumble into December.
Exactly when will our family be dissolved?
Will our holidays be quiet
instead of tentatively still?
Will we go, on Christmas afternoon, to visit my brother
in some highly staffed refuge
like the ones I read about online last night?

Will Steven's first real holiday gift to us
be his absence from our home,
and is that a present I will ever be able to want?

"O come ye to Bethlehem."

I try to keep the tears in my eyes, away from the music,
but a sharp sound escapes from my horn.
Cal doesn't quite stare at me over his bari;
he has to keep glancing down
at the music he's close to memorizing.
His eyes flitting my way make me look, for some reason,
out the interior window
to see the unmistakable back of Dave's shaggy head,
the edge of a book.
Is he waiting for me?
And wouldn't that have made a perfect morning
not so very long,
long ago?

53

Mr. Orson sets down his baton,
like a razor slicing my fifty-five minutes of ragtime bliss
off the top of the day.

The end of the music hurts.
Slowly, slowly,
I slide the mouthpiece from the lead pipe,
rub the cleaning cloth over my brass companion,
set the trumpet into its velvet-lined case,
click the buckles shut.

Through the window, I can see the top half of Dave.
He is doggedly tapping something into his cell phone,
but every minute or so, his head straightens,
he looks toward the band room door.

"Comin' to homeroom?" Cal asks.
He heaves his bari case up onto the shelf,
reaches for mine.

"Thanks." I hand it to him.

"Got a lot of art on this thing." He smiles
at the custom square declaring,
"Up with Jazz; Down with People"
that adorns the case's center;
my glitter-enhanced black-and-white sticker
of Dizzy Gillespie
blowing into his horn in all his full-cheeked glory.
"It's cool."

"Thanks."
Through the window,
I see Dave glance toward the band room door
one last time.
Watch with something like relief
as he shoves his phone into his pocket
and walks down the hall.

I want and don't want
to feel his carelessly strong embrace around my ribs,
his lips on my lips.
My heart is so heavy, my eyes too close to tears
to dare try and explain
why I ran from him in the parking lot,
if I even know myself beyond my overdeveloped instinct
to slip from tight grips that, at home, signal only danger.

"Let's go see what Mrs. Pendleton's wearing today, Cal."

54

"It's yoga tonight, isn't it?"
Justine meets me at the lockers,
bumps her shoulder against mine.

"Yeah," I breathe.

"Wanna meet up after orchestra tomorrow, then?
We could check out that new jewelry store downtown."

"I've got a music lesson," I say.
I want to tell her that pretty soon,
I won't have to race home anymore,
that we can shop any day after school,
have sleepovers, go to dances like normal friends.
But I am afraid.
Afraid she'll be sorry.
Afraid she'll be glad.
Afraid she'll feel all the things I feel
but say them out loud, like Justine always can.
Though, usually, Justine's bravery
makes me feel stronger, I am afraid
that, right now, her words

will be nails digging into my scabbed-over heart,
making me bleed.

55

I can't bring myself to go home at three o'clock.
Instead, I find Dave
sitting on the bleachers behind the school,
a lighter in one hand, burning tiny bits of paper,
watching smoke rise toward the clouds.

I ignore the tick-ticking of my watch
counting down the minutes to yoga.
I bury the humiliation I still feel from our last parting
beneath the horror of last night.
I reach for the lighter.

He lets go, surprised but not unyielding.
Watches as I take from my backpack
the sheet music to "Adeste Fideles"
and set it ablaze.

The pages are dry, curling quickly to brown ash.
I squeal, drop the burning sheaves
onto the gravel at our feet,
desperately try to stomp out the forest fire
I see in my imagination.

He laughs.

"Don't laugh!" My back is to him, feet still stamping.

"Why're you burning stuff you might need?"
He's taken the lighter back now,
flicking again and again, small, harmless flames,
no longer touching them to paper.

"I don't owe you an explanation."
I can't decide whether I'm staying or going, so I lean
against the dented silver metal of the bleacher bench,
feel a ridge of cool press into my backside,
try to look righteously angry.

"You're something, Daisy Meehan." He chuckles.
"Something else."

"And you're not?"
(Sometimes I say the absolutely dumbest things.)

"I dunno.
You didn't seem to think much of me the other day."

"That wasn't . . . I didn't . . ."
I feel my face burning,

bend away from the cool bench, reach down
to pick up a wayward chunk of scorched sheet music.
"You going to The Movie House tonight?"

Dave flicks the lighter even faster,
little flames like hopes being lit and dashed
in fractions of seconds.
"Nah," he says. Nothing more. Just flames.

My mind turns white.
I cannot figure out why I am standing here before Dave;
I just know I am angry
and it feels like Dave, with his leather and tousle,
his carelessness and fire,
is someone I could be angry with, HBO-style.

The phone in the back pocket of my jeans starts to buzz:
a "hurry up" text from Mom
that makes me want to linger.

"Remember when we were in kindergarten, Dave?"
I point past the bleachers,
past the fence to the park swings just beyond.
"We used to play space explorers over on those swings."

"You always had to be ship captain."
He grins. "Still do, I guess."

I am overwhelmed with longing to touch him,
to tell him what's going on in my house,
to ask him why we stopped being friends and when, exactly,
those seams came undone,
to ask him about his dad and his little half-sisters,
for the details of the things I have heard about his life
from the small-town grapevine
that twists around us.

"I wish we were little again."
I turn my shoulder,
don't want him to see my eyes grow wet.

"Sometimes . . . ," he says. "Sometimes I do, too."

"But we're not.
And I've gotta go home and watch my brother."

56

"Deadlines Amuse Me,"
says a yellow handmade ceramic tile
relaxing on an embellished wire plate stand
on the kitchen counter.

"You're late." Mom is pacing before the fridge,
the carefree quotation at her back,
her soft pastel yoga clothes
belied by the frown lines around her mouth,
the creases by her eyes,
the way she attacks the dishes in the sink.

"I'm here, aren't I?"

I turn to Steven, who's already got Blokus open,
nothing left of his cookies but crumbs.

"Want to play, Steven?"
He keeps laying out game pieces as if I haven't spoken,
neat, even lines of plastic, getting ready.
But there's an edge to his order,

his rhythm just slightly faster than it should be.
If it were an ordinary day, I'd be on eggshells already,
waiting for the explosion.
Now, I almost want the dam to burst.

"When are you going to tell him?" I ask Mom.
"How are you going to explain . . . ?"

She hangs her apron on the hook by the pantry door,
smooths her T-shirt over her flat stomach.
I count the rises and falls
of her pronounced collarbones.
"Careful," she says.

We both look at Steven.
The game is ready. Now he waits.

"I'll play," I say to no one in particular.

"Dad is working late. He'll be home in time to put—"

"I know."

I nudge the first blue piece toward Steven's hand,
hear the door close softly behind our mother.

57

I fumble to answer the ten thirty ring of my cell.
"You will not believe this!"
Justine's shriek practically explodes the phone.
There are no rules about quiet after dark
in her just-mom-and-me household.

"Won't believe what?"

"Ned Hoffman just asked me on a date for tomorrow night.
He said a *date*, like we were in the 1950s."

"I haven't gotten that far in A-PUSH.
Is that what they called the antiquated
one-boy-one-girl-one-meal evening?"

"Better than attack-kissing against a Ford Fiesta, right?"

She can joke because I didn't—couldn't—
really tell Justine how it felt,
how much I can't stop thinking about that afternoon.
I just told her Dave owed me dinner first.

"You're gonna kiss Ned Hoffman," I singsong.

"I might," Justine says. "He's . . . well, kind of earnest,
but he's cute enough."

"And we know he'll be a gentleman," I tease back.

"I want a boyfriend.
The Black-and-White Dance isn't far away."

"This is preparation for the school formal?"
My giggling shriek almost matches Justine's.

"Maybe you could ask Dave," Justine says.

Mom taps at my door,
enters without waiting for permission.
"Daisy, it's getting a little too loud," she says.
"Don't wake up Steven."

"I'm sorry."
I watch Mom's skeleton fingers
slide around the doorknob,
imagine them on Steven's shoulders,
guiding his guileless form away

from our front door, our home,
forever.
I tune down my voice to a whisper.
"I gotta go, Justine."

"But we haven't even talked about what I should wear!
Come over after your trumpet lesson tomorrow
afternoon and help me choose."

"I will." My voice, still soft, as deceptively ordinary
as this night.

58

"Daisy." Mom sets a glass of juice beside my cereal bowl
at breakfast.
"Your dad and I were wondering . . .
well, you haven't said how you feel
about our plan for Steven."

I look at the tumbler, not her face.
It's safely acrylic, with a tasteful dimpled pattern
that mimics cut crystal. And tinted blue,
which makes the orange juice inside look faintly green.

I slide my hand around to the cup.
The ticking of the watch on my wrist
reaches into my ears, persistent, wiry,
so loud I wonder if Mom can hear it, too.
"I guess I haven't," I say, drawing my lip to the rim,
gulping the liquid to prevent more words
from spilling out.

Should I care
that Mom never offers to toast me a waffle
like she does for Steven every day?

We're a house of three parents, one child.
I think Mom and Dad have seen it this way
for a long time. Me too, I guess.
But right now, I wish someone would tie my shoes,
cut my food,
not ask for my consent
to this enormous, terrifying choice they have made.

I have no idea
if I should build them some bridge to acquiescence,
offer some way for this to be right.

Like I carry my parents' history,
I carry this future plan—
a crippling weight
that seems to have slowed the beat of my heart.
I am walking eternally through a kitchen of quicksand
littered with brochures
for Alternatives Academy, Regis House
photo-illustrated with the scrubbed-clean faces,
brushed-back hair
of oversize, well-kept, eternal children
setting a table, folding clothes,
glancing up from a small bed of garden soil.

My smartphone registers an e-mail from

Overton Academy,
letting me know that my recommendation
has been received,
my application is complete.

I hit "delete,"
collect my stuff for Youth Orchestra,
wave to Dad behind his paper, Mom at her sink,
Steven, my only brother.

59

Youth Orchestra is easy for me.
Sixty-odd familiar faces, just a few
as musically accomplished as I am, just a few
boys whose faces my eyes linger on, just a few
friends I've made in the years we've shared
Saturday mornings together.
We are concert comrades,
connecting only outside the realms
of our private and academic lives,
though there is one other girl from my school:
Shelby, who's in my math class
but doesn't play in any ensembles at Evergreen.
She's sat in the NHSYA flute second chair
as long as I've been first trumpet,
yet we've never carpooled or crushed on the same boy,
barely ever spoken
despite our common school, our years together.

Shelby the Asperger's girl
(though I think they might not call it that anymore):
diligent, distant, somehow different.

I used to wince, watching her attempts to befriend,
as if her "mainstream" classmates would let her in,
as if we—or she—really understood the emotion
behind our rejections.
I'd sigh with relief that Steven was safely out of the mainstream,
would never have to endure this kind of floating
through a world politely tolerating, never really trying to know him.
Now, I wish, wish, *wish*
Shelby's life
for my brother.

I smile at her
as I disassemble my trumpet, wipe it down.
Her eyes startle behind her glasses before
she smiles back.

60

From practice
I go straight to my private trumpet lesson
with Aggie Nedrum
at the music school housed in the same arts complex
where the orchestra rehearses.

Outside Aggie's studio door,
I'm surprised by the face of Cal O'Casey.
He's got two instrument cases:
the bari and something smaller,
probably a tenor sax.

"Hey there, Daisy," he says.

"You taking lessons with Aggie?" I ask.
I feel strangely offended,
don't want to share my teacher.
"How'd you find her?"

"I asked Mr. Orson who you study with,
because you're the best musician in our band."

He isn't fawning or flattering but almost businesslike,
folder of music tucked beneath his arm,
unable to hide the faint smile of satisfaction I often sport
after a good lesson with Aggie.
"I just started t'day. She's good."
He gives a funny little salute.

"Yeah," I say, watching him walk to the elevator,
his stride light, happy.

Do I watch too many people walk away?
Cal? Dave?
Dad from Mom?
Will I watch Ned lead Justine down a path
away from our friendship?

I think I am good at this—
standing in the wake of departures.
Like eating hot lunch, I acquiesce, accept
what is dumped onto life's tray before me,
even try to enjoy the bland potatoes, flavorless soups.
I allow people to simply exit doors,
never invite them in.

Yet despite Mom and Dad's well-reasoned arguments,
my own secret plans to escape from home
for the summer,

and my million silent wishes
for a different life, something stirs in me
when I picture them sending Steven away.
I do not know if I can eat from this dish,
if I can celebrate this freedom.

Like a Civil War soldier pitted against his own kin,
I know I cannot merely watch this plot unfold,
that I must take my own stand.
Even if my greatest rebellion until now
has been flicking the channel
from the Cartoon Network to HBO,
even if I'm not sure what is right
or how to make myself heard,
I cannot just let Steven go.

61

"Hi, Daisy, how was orchestra?"
Aggie opens her studio door at my knock,
pushes up her sleeves. I see
the trickling lines of tattooed flowers,
music notes, and tangled vines
that end just below her elbows.

I used to meet with Aggie every week,
but school and bands and competitions and growing up
and Steven got in the way and now
it's only two or three lessons a month,
squeezed in with a bit of luck.

I'm likely the last student she'll see today
before heading down to Boston to play a nighttime gig.
Aggie is badass
in a totally different way from Dave Miller.
She looks like a pit girl, tatted and ringed—
not so much eyeliner, though—
and bleached-white hair shorn close to her scalp.
She can play any brass thing with a valve—hell,

practically anything made of metal:

trumpet,

coronet,

French horn,

sax.

A year or two ago, she said,
"There's nothing left I can teach you, Daisy.
You should go down to the Conservatory in Boston
or over to Portsmouth to study with one of the teachers
at the U."

But Mom and Dad couldn't go looking
for some fancy teacher for their musically gifted girl.
Any energy they might've had for that
was spent on Internet searches
for teaching autistics to verbalize, for specialists, doctors—
flashing online dreams, visions of some kind of better day,
better week for their boy; for them.
A night of uninterrupted sleep
or just some daylight moments
with enough safety to simply sit and be still.

And I had known all of this
in the instant it took to tear my glance
away from Aggie's, drop it down to the music stand, and say,

"I don't think my parents could manage that,"
in a voice I've learned to use that's clear and firm:
don't-pity-me yet uncontestable.
There are things you learn from living like I do.

"How about you play me the Ellington piece?"
she asks now, rubbing her hands together
as if she were getting ready for Thanksgiving dinner.
I love that Aggie loves to hear me play.
It makes the music all about the joy of sharing,
not the advantages of escape.

I lift my horn to my lips,
release my desperation into the purity of sound.

62

"So, Justine and Ned, sittin' in a tree?"
I squeeze between two pairs of jeans and a pile
of sweaters sprawled across the rose chenille bedspread
that is also playing host to half a dozen pairs of shoes.

"K-i-s-s-i . . ." Justine stops, mid-rhyme,
to smear her lips with silvery pink.
"You like?"

"That color should be called Sexy Robot!"
I throw a metallic gray sweater in her direction.
It is the fourth lipstick shade, the sixth outfit
my usually decisive friend has tried.

"Take that, Callum O'Casey!"
Justine cinches her waist with a dark blue belt.

"You only ever liked his accent anyway."

"But he can be such an ass. It just pisses me off."

"I saw him at the music school today," I tell her.
"He's started lessons with Aggie."

Justine doesn't say anything else, just turns sideways.
She has a thin waist and the jeans-sweater-belt combo
looks great, especially finished with high-heeled boots.
It's the kind of look I could never pull off.
It'd look too studied, like I was playing dress-up.
Besides, I'd feel naked
without a pair of customized Keds on my feet.

"You look amazing.
Ned is going to seriously drop his teeth."
An unexpected wave of jealousy passes through me.

"He has a nice smile, I think."

It's weird to see Justine so tentative about a guy
she used to call "Ernie Earnest"
when we whispered about him in class,
while I called him "Judgie McJudgment."

Some memories are better left in the past,
some thoughts unspoken.

And maybe Justine is right
to be thinking about the Black-and-White Dance
already.

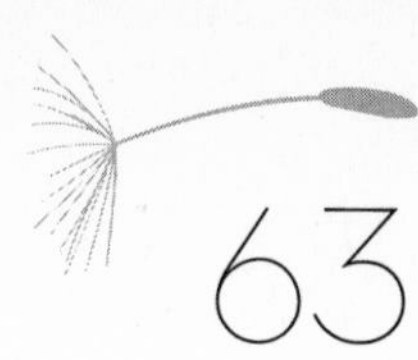

63

I leave at seven,
half an hour before Ned is due at Justine's door.
I cannot imagine that any HBO warnings
need to precede their date. More easily,
I can picture myself ninja-kicking Ned's straight teeth
as he talks about his volunteer work with special-needs kids,
his eyes cast politely downward,
away from me and what he knows of my brother.
Ned is the darling of the PTA-mom crowd,
likes to wear a thin tie
and a dress shirt with sleeves rolled up
to show he's ready to work.

Why shouldn't Justine have a good boy?

The question guides my car
past the Main Street turnoff for home
to the town park.
I pull into the lot by the pits,
look for a black-and-red Fiesta, a dark, tousled head.

He's over there, leaning against a picnic table.
My hands still on the wheel,
I watch girls and boys drink from bottles,
laugh and shove—easy movements, as if they were
dancing to unheard music.
Beyond, the lake is a glassy black foreground
to a live painting of pine and oak trees, nearby mountains:
a spectacular, dark tableau that
I think has somehow managed to stop time in this place.

If time stood still, there would be
no history to study,
no need to watch Steven,
no ominous institution to visit,
no guilt.

I put the car in park, turn off the ignition, wish for a second
I were wearing pink lipstick and boots with heels,
but all I've got are my sneakers and a blue fleece
that, I think, looks nice with my eyes.
I unclip the barrette,
shake my hair loose down my back,
step out onto the pavement.

About ten paces before I reach him,
Dave catches sight of me.

"You coming to invite me to The Movie House?"

"I thought maybe I'd take a taste of Belden's brew."

Dave's eyes widen a little.
"We've just got Natty Bo tonight."

"That's okay." I put up my chin,
imagining Ned Hoffman holding the door for Justine
outside La Parisienne,
the fancy place he reserved for their dinner.
Beside the picnic bench is a cooler of ice and beer bottles.
I grab one. "Have an opener?"

He laughs. "Twist-off."
But he takes the bottle from my hand,
removes the cap, passes it back.

"Look who's here!" Josh Belden joins us at the cooler.
His hand is in the back pocket
of one of the nose-ringed girls I recognize from school.
She's new this year, I know, because most of us
have been together since we were six years old.
Most of us remember every win and loss:
my skirt-stuck-in-tights humiliation,
the time Dave got sent to the principal

for bringing a slingshot to school in third grade,
how Josh used to cry every time he struck out in baseball.
We've signed each other's wrist and ankle casts,
attended grandparents' funerals,
spun the bottle in so many basements
that we've pretty much all kissed.

The new girl's name is Liese, and she doesn't know
about Josh's old tears,
or that Dave and I had marriage plans
before we lost our baby teeth.
"Hey there." She raises her beer in greeting,
looping a possessive arm around Josh's neck.

"Hi." I steel myself and take a sip.
The taste of dirt mixed with seltzer floods my mouth.

"You can eat that disgusting tomato soup at school
but you wince at a beer?" Dave teases.

"It's . . . fine. It's good."
Josh and Liese, Mark and Marielle,
and a few other uncoupled girls and guys laugh,
but in a friendly way.
I hope I don't look as wide-eyed, as uncertain as I feel,
suddenly jealous of all the nights they've spent listening

to the lapping lake, huddling together
in the chill freedom of not practicing music
or giving their parents a "break."

"I'm glad you came, Daisy."

I gasp as his beer-chilled fingers wrap around mine.
He tugs me gently away from the group,
toward the water's edge.

"Remember . . . ?" My voice sounds airy,
all my breath still busily reacting
to the tingling coolness of Dave Miller's hand.
When I picture him in my mind,
we are both small, sandboxed, smiling,
fearless, without question
of what would happen
after we finished our make-believe.
"Remember eating jelly sandwiches?"

"I still hate peanut butter!"

Now my breath whooshes out,
all of me pulsing with gladness,
maybe even thankful to Ned Hoffman
for whatever role he played

in guiding my Subaru here tonight.

"Come on." Dave says.
We reach the water's edge.
The tide has pushed a ridge of driftwood
and fallen pine needles onto the sand.
I shiver.
Dave reaches his muscled arm across my back,
his hand dangling over my shoulder.
Step, step, step.
We're a little out of sync—his stride longer than mine,
a jazz hesitation,
trying to keep time with the lapping waves.

Water seeps above the thin rubber soles
into the canvas of my Keds.
I imagine the stamp ink dyeing my toes purple and
shiver again.

Belden and the gang are out of sight.
We're at another clearing, a solo picnic bench
devoid of knife marks,
the ground clear of bottle caps, butts,
the detritus of the pits.
Perhaps it's on private property,
belongs to the folks whose boat dock I see just ahead,

or the log cabin up the hill,
its darkened windows suggesting it's just a vacation spot,
unoccupied now.

Dave slides his arm from my shoulder.
Without worry of trespassing (or maybe just not caring),
he climbs onto the tabletop, not the bench,
beckons with his eyes.
I scramble up beside him.

"Look up," he says.

I lean back on my elbows,
watch minute flecks of yellow starlight
fight the blackness of space.
Inhale the lakeside air's aroma of damp temptation.

"Now, some honor roll guy might try to tell you
the names of the constellations." He laughs.
"But you know me better than that, Daisy-brains."

"Do I?" The question flickers from my lips.

"You know I'd never try some line on you."

"No, you just trek me along a dark beach

until my feet are soaked!"
My giggle turns into a nervous shudder.

What I do know
is being here with Dave has managed to let me forget
my music school applications, my parents, Steven.
I've been following the music of the moment,
immersed in the exhilarating, terrifying improvisation
that is me tonight.

"Sorry about that." Dave jumps off the picnic top.
I worry that time will start again. But no.
He slips off my Keds and sets them on the bench,
rubs my damp feet with his hands,
shrugs out of his dark hoodie
and wraps it around my naked toes.

"Aren't you cold?"

I feel his answer
in the electricity that ripples through my body
as Dave lies down beside me on the rough tabletop.
He tangles his fingers into my hair,
turns my face toward his.
His kiss is softer than before.
This time, I push my lips against his,

relax the strong, controlled muscles of my face.
He exhales warm breath that curls around my cheeks.
I sigh, wanting only more,
more kisses that aren't just dreams.

Dave reaches under my fleece,
toying with the waistband of my jeans.
Then his hands move higher,
sliding along my stomach, over my breast.
He sighs with a strange urgency,
and I feel a mixture of want and fear
as I close my eyes to the stars above us.

64

"Miller? Miller! Where the . . . ?"
Josh Belden is hollering from the shore.
"You're my ride, man!"

"Keep your shit together.
I'll be right there." Dave sits up, shaking his head.

In the dark, I feel myself blush,
scramble to fix my fleece, reach for my shoes.
"Where is my other . . . ?"

Dave pulls his lighter from his pocket.
The small flame guides us to my left Ked,
fallen beneath the table.

"Let's go."
He takes my hand
and guides me back through the dark with such ease
I wonder how many girls have made this walk with him.
Right now, I don't care.
My body is alive with feeling,
not thought, not plans, not worries.

I cannot make out Belden's expression in the dark,
don't know
if it's surprise or maybe a quick congrats to Dave
for getting some from the trumpet girl.

"My car's just up there."
I turn away, the good girl in me afraid
that any more time with Dave
would certainly turn up the movie rating.
Blushing as I realize I don't think I would mind.

"Hey, wait." Dave pulls me back,
brushes his lips over mine.

"Uh, thanks," I say,
now certain that being kissed that way has not made me
less stupid.

"See ya, Daisy." Belden waves.
He and Dave get into the Fiesta.

In the Subaru, I clip my hair back into a ponytail,
don't bother to check the time before I start the ignition.

65

Into silence so pure I can hear well-oiled hinges sigh
as the front door swings open, I creep
down the empty hall.
Is anyone in this house?
Have Mom and Dad already spirited Steven away?
No, they are sitting side by side on the living room couch,
eyes furious.

"Do you know what time it is?"
Dad's icy voice splinters the stillness.

"We called Justine. She said you left hours ago.
She's on a date, but she said for you to call as soon . . ."
Mom clutches wads of tissues in each hand;
her skin is splotched from scrubbing at tears.
"Margaret-Mary Meehan. We were so worried!"

"Don't you think we have enough on our hands
without you pulling something like this?"
Dad smacks his palms against his knees, stands up,
stalks to the stairs.

"Where were you?" Mom whispers.

They shouldn't want my answer.
Anywhere but here.
Making out with a boy.
Somewhere I could make time stand still.

Beneath my fleece and jeans,
my skin is hot with the memory of Dave's touch.
More intoxicated by my fleeting taste of freedom
than if I'd drunk a gallon of that disgusting beer.
I am flying above responsibility, above guilt.
My chilled fingers wad to fists.

"Oh, sorry, Mom.
Were you and Dad wanting to go out tonight?
Did I leave you without a babysitter?"

"You know that's not what I meant."
Her thin hands tremble as she wipes her eyes again.

"What do you mean, then?" I ask,
but don't stay to hear the answer.
In the hallway, I pull my phone from my bag,
text Justine: "Home safe.

Sorry if my mom freaked u out.
More in the morning."

My purple feet squish in my ruined shoes
as I follow my father's path up the stairs.

66

My parents haven't tried to bring Steven to church
in months of Sundays, long ago abandoning any notion
that faith could guide them to cure, or acceptance,
or even the ability to forgive themselves
for the life we live.

Now, from my bedroom window, I watch them,
Dad guiding Steven by the arm, ignoring
his repeated attempts to shrug out of blazer and tie;
Mom smiling, trying to keep her movements calm.

Even after the car has been out of sight a long time
I still stand before the glass,
my hair wet from a long shower
that didn't quite manage to rinse away
the inky evidence of last night—
a memory that makes me shiver, makes me want.

67

"Justine's coming for dinner," Mom says
the second my family comes through the door.
"I invited her at church."

"Seriously, Mom?"
I press my pale, purple feet
against the metal rungs of the kitchen barstool.
"What if Steven . . . ?"

"Dad will be here.
It might be nice for you to have some company."

She opens her mouth
as if to say something more,
but her lips just close.
She goes to the fridge,
starts pulling out salad greens, lemons,
while I imagine the bitter taste of her unspoken words,
some promise about how, soon, invitations to friends
won't have to be planned
around the availability of protection.

Another ironic magnet on Mom's refrigerator is the old saw,
"If life gives you lemons . . ."
But what if you cannot divide your life
between the sour and the sweet?
What if you kiss a boy you loved as a child
but can no longer name the emotions you feel
as you press into his lips,
let his hot fingers roam, drink in only the desire
to lose yourself in anyone else?
What if the elation that fills your heart when you think
of not having to care for your brother
also stops it beating entirely—
from grief? From guilt?
From some other emotion you don't know how to name?

"I don't need company."
I stalk past the family room
where Dad has planted Steven, now watching cartoons;
tiptoe up the stairs to my room,
where the history book open on my desk confronts me.

Are all people "created equal"?
Do they have equal rights to freedom?
Thanks, A-PUSH Civil War unit,
you blasted annoying class,

for shining a light on these questions that,
whether framed by race, religion, or ability
to communicate, seem reflected in Lincoln's words.

I've learned about men whose sons and brothers died
fighting for the Union.
Yet while they mourned, they were still opposed
to freeing the slaves,
could believe nothing more than that their loved ones
died in vain.

Who should sacrifice freedom so others can be free?
I doubt those early Americans ever imagined a scenario
of a family enslaved by a boy
who is himself a prisoner of his own mind.

What might freedom be for Steven?
Before my parents send him away, I want my brother
to tell me what he wants.
Like I want things I see on television movies,
where actors find resolutions that real people never see.

68

My phone buzzes.
"Ned asked me to the Black-and-White Dance!"
Justine texts.

"With pink flowers?" I text back.

"Hee-hee. Tell u more at dinner."

I hesitate before typing my reply.
"You don't have to come tonight. I'll understand."

There is no beat before her words fly back. "I'm coming!"

I dare anyone to try to tell me Justine isn't brave.

I close the history book,
imagine choosing the blue or the gray uniform
of a Northern or Southern Civil War soldier—
simple, subdued colors that spoke volumes,
pitted brother against brother.
My heart weeps for those long dead,
those broken families,

as the ghostly Mason-Dixon Line
that divides my family's house
from the rest of Jasper,
from school, from melody,
rises with sudden clarity in my mind.

I wonder if my parents see it?
If Justine feels her feet stepping over it
when she dares cross our threshold?
Whether Steven's tripping gait as he makes his way
down our front walkway
is a struggle with this border?

There's a track on Miles Davis's iconic album
called "Blue in Green."
I blast it through my earbuds, straining to find
in the trumpet's probing, rising-and-fading,
dissolving-and-emerging trail
over the piano's soft chords, bass's warm thrum,
a path to join black and white—
to envision a world that doesn't have two sides.

Is there a way to tear down the fence, mend the divide
between
daughter and parents,
autistic and "normal,"

silence and music,

home and life?

69

I don't come downstairs until our softly modified
doorbell rings,
announcing the arrival of Justine.

We eat sautéed shrimp over capellini pasta, on square
blue plates Mom found at an Italian import store
that almost perfectly match
the tiles in the kitchen backsplash.

Dad tops off Mom's wine.
I watch jealously.
I am cold sober as the pebbles on the bottom of a lake,
pushed and pulled by a current,
not responsible for their direction
or if they bruise the soles of some barefoot girl
walking, jeans rolled up,
beside some boy.

Late-afternoon sun fills the room with a surreal haze.
Justine and I clink our water goblets, twist our forks
through strands of boiled semolina, tender seafood,

while Steven eats his room-temp macaroni and cheese;
and the words from our mouths are about
the gorgeous colors of the fall leaves,
the "we never make it to the lake enough in summer"
that makes me think again of Dave.

70

Do they not care where I was last night?
I am still waiting for an inquisition at least as intense
as when I ask to borrow twenty dollars;
some kind of admonishment, or punishment,
as if I weren't a third adult in this house
but the actual teen that I am.
The one time that maybe they would be right
to stop me . . . they don't.

Instead, Dad leads Steven to the family room television
while Justine and I help with the dishes.

And the only question Mom asks is,
"Do you girls want dessert?"

"Oh, that's all right, Mrs. Meehan," Justine says.

"Yeah," I add hurriedly.
I don't want Mom to thank Justine for coming over,
say she understands her nervousness.
I'm not ready for anyone to know

my parents' new plan for Steven.
"It's still early.
I was thinking Justine and I could go to the mall."

"That's a half-hour drive. Don't you have to practice trumpet later?" Mom says.

"Suddenly, you want to involve yourself in my practice schedule? You haven't even asked me
where I was last night!"
I throw the dish towel onto the countertop,
grab the Subaru keys from the hook by the refrigerator.
"Let's go."

Justine's eyes widen, but she goes to get her coat.
I don't turn around to check my mother's expression,
like I didn't turn around
after I told Dave I couldn't go to The Movie House.

71

"Are we really going to the mall?" Justine asks
as I idle at the four-way stop
where Broad Street crosses Main.

"It's probably too far." I think guiltily of my trumpet,
despite the scene I made at home.
I drive past Bouchard's and down the steep hill
to Jasper's humble downtown:
a block-long strip featuring a grocery store, a gas station,
the town library,
and a surprisingly large Walgreens.
"Let's go here."

We pass Ashleigh Anderson and our Evergreen Wolves
quarterback exiting as we enter.
As contrary as we are proud, Jasper folks enjoy a bargain
as much as they dislike a chain store.
The result: Sunday shopping at Walgreens is so common
I am surprised
not to see half of my class wandering the aisles.

"So . . . this is just a little retail therapy."
Justine gives me one of her
if-she-wasn't-my-best-friend-I'd-think-she-was-angry
"fess up" looks.

"It's been a long week." I try not to sound too dark,
too selfish. "You never finished telling me
what happened with Ned."

Our heads bent together,
since you never know who's in the next Walgreens aisle,
she whispers, "He said he knew the dance wasn't until
next month, but he had such a great time at dinner
and . . . I told him yes.
Oh, and that I was glad he asked early,
so I have plenty of time to shop for a dress!"

I should be happy for her, but all I can wonder
is if Justine is settling for Judgie McJudgment,
Ernie Earnest; whether he is still the boy who laughed
instead of telling me to fix my skirt,
or whether he has changed.
Maybe I'm just jealous
that everything is happening for my friend
like a charming black-and-white movie—
dinner date, then dance invitation—

instead of the thing I have with Dave:
making out without dating; beer before wine.

I smile. "A pink dress, of course."

We have woven our way to the cosmetics section.
I inspect a burgundy eye pencil,
take a bottle of navy-blue nail polish from a shelf.

Justine takes my selections from my hands.
"Did something happen with Dave? Are you okay?"

"Of course I'm okay. We kissed.
A lot. But it was good. I'm fine."

"Then why the dark makeup?"

"I kind of feel like shaking things up," I answer.

"Well, you'll sure look more like Dave's crowd with this.
Let's go back to my house.
My mom hates all my candy-colored shadows.
She'll love doing your eyes."

72

I am the brag-about-her daughter who blithely acquiesces
to schedules, colors circumscribed by Mom and Dad.
Until Dave.
Until now.
If it's ordinary they want,
then maybe I should transform
into something far less
than the outstanding musician I am,
show them that sending Steven away
will not turn our house into any kind of paradise.

I pull into Justine's driveway.
Inside, we sit beneath a swirly chandelier,
on chic satin dressing table chairs,
elbows resting on the coral granite counter
in the giant master bathroom.

As she uncaps the eyeliner pencil I bought,
Shirley, Justine's mother, gives me one of her *looks*,
like maybe Mom's already told her
some of what's going on,

or maybe it's just that she's known me so long,
she can read my emotions
as well as her own daughter's.
"Look down, honey."
She pencils black lines around my eyes,
smudging with the side of her pinkie finger;
brushes on a layer of gray eye shadow.
"Here, you can mascara your own lashes."

"Maybe that's a little dark for school," Justine suggests.

"We're not at school," I say.

"But it's a school night," Shirley reminds us.
"Another half hour and you should head home."

In the gilt-framed mirror
I see a girl who isn't quite me—
instead, something more arresting, abstract,
like the word *sorry*,
the skull beneath the skin.
I hope this face is braver, more certain of things.
"I'm gonna try the nail polish."

I unscrew the bottle,
wrinkle my nose at the stinging vinegar aroma,

glad Steven isn't near to smell this offense.
The thick liquid spreads cold over my fingernails.
I paint imperfectly, tagging my fingertips,
coating my cuticles, as I darken each left-hand digit.
Switch awkwardly to paint my right hand,
which comes out even worse than the left.

"I could help," Justine offers.

"No, I want to learn how to do this."

My fingers twitch as I wait for the stuff to dry.
Shirley returns the makeup to the Walgreens bag,
steps back to study her makeover handiwork.
"That dark liner really pops the blue of your eyes."

In Jasper, everybody thinks Shirley wears
too much makeup,
too little else;
that maybe the too-much of her
was what drove her husband away.
Justine pretends she doesn't care,
shows her allegiance to her mother
with shocking high heels.
But maybe Ned is some kind of counterbalance,

buttoned-up, crisp,
town-approved,
fulfilling her secret dreams of a future
in unscandalous pastels.

73

It's late when I get home,
but I go to the basement to practice anyway—
half glad, half sorry Mom and Dad aren't awake
to see my new look.

I play the gentlest part of the Hummel concerto,
the one that calmed my brother; wonder
what the trumpet will mean, how it will live in my life,
when he is gone.

74

"Aggie is an amazing teacher, isn't—"
Cal O'Casey begins a sentence he doesn't finish,
taken aback, perhaps, by the black of my sweatshirt,
the Keds I carefully covered last night
with brown skeletons and squares of dark green,
the thick kohl lines around my eyes.

Even the unflappable Mrs. Pendleton pauses at my desk
en route to the front of the classroom.
I don't need judgment from someone wearing
a barely-acceptably-teacher-length skirt,
just turn my raccoon eyes away.

Justine sighs.
"Just in time for me to start dating Ned,
you turn into Goth Girl."

"Hope I don't wreck your chances in the student council
election." Words I meant to sound teasing
come out with a bitter edge
that freezes Justine's smile.

"Yeah, well . . ."
is all she says before Ned arrives, walks to her desk
with a proprietary saunter that makes me wonder
if the two of them did even more
than Dave and me on Friday night.

"Sorry, Daisy, I'm a bit confused," Cal says.
"Is Justine running for student office?"

At the front of the room,
Mrs. Pendleton stoops to pick up a pencil,
which makes a few of the boys inhale audibly.
To her right, I see Shelby, already sitting down,
pushing her notebook into alignment
with the edge of her desk.

"Nah," I say halfheartedly to Cal,
my eyes fixed on Shelby but seeing Steven,
imagining what it might be like for him
in a classroom like this.
"What were you saying about Aggie?"

"She's a bit of all right, i'n't she?
The way she plays a horn."

Cal is looking past me now,
to a vision of Aggie, the musician in her,
just like I'm looking past him to a dream of my brother.
And I see in my mind's eye Steven's gaze:
distant, distracted, like both of us now.
Maybe he, too, is always looking for some faraway thing
that makes perfect sense inside his head;
it's just that he can't tell anybody.

"She charges a lot," Cal continues,
"but the Ackermans are letting me earn money
by raking their leaves—and I'll shovel their driveway
when the snow starts—
so I can pay.
She's worth it."

I look hard, maybe for the first time,
at Cal's holey jeans, worn brown shoes, and think
maybe he's no more ordinary-middle-class than I;
that maybe there are secrets behind his quiet smile,
reasons for the passion that throbs through his bari
like I've never heard before.

I try to remember how many different shirts I've seen
him wear,
can count only three.

Tally in my mind the price of the myriad matching sets
of Nike and adidas sweats and tees Mom buys for Steven,
sporting graphics of bats he will never swing,
baskets he will never make.
He likes smooth fabrics,
elastic-waist pants that require no belting,
adapt to his increasing size.
I think Mom likes the way that, from the back,
the outfits make him look pretty much like a normal,
chubby guy.

I shake myself back into the conversation with Cal.
"Aggie's definitely worth it."
My voice comes out surprisingly soft.

75

Halfway through A-PUSH I realize
Dave has not texted me since Saturday night,
when I let him do those things,
when I did those things with him.

The North battles the South
in Mr. Angelli's clipped New England monologue,
an accent that somehow lacks the drama or passion
I imagine for war
or love.
My mind drifts to an HBO moment.
I play back me and Dave on the bench by the lake,
only this time my hair is longer,
my shoes are three-inch stilettos,
and Dave . . .
Dave says words like "you're beautiful" and "I love you"
and "I'll call you before you even make it home."
I am lost in Adult Content and breathing fast
when the people around me start to shuffle, pile books.
Some sound in my fantasy must have been the real zing
of the bell.

Mr. Angelli and Cal stand over me.
I wonder if they can hear
the skittering of my horny heart.

"Daisy," Mr. Angelli begins,
oblivious to the mess before him.
"Cal here is having a bit of trouble mastering our
American history, so I'd like you to work with him
on the next project: writing a short autobiography
of a fictional Civil War–era slave."

"Er, a slave?" I murmur doltishly.

"Cal has the reading list and the details."
Mr. Angelli points to a paper in Cal's hand,
gives me a nod, expecting no resistance.

Despite my dangerous
new nails-and-sneakers color scheme,
it doesn't occur to me to resist anyway.

76

"P'raps we can meet up after school today,"
Cal suggests.

"I, um, babysit on Mondays," I tell him.
"How about tomorrow?"

"Okay. Say, the library at three, then?"

It's a logical place and time.
Cal can't know that Dave and I
kind of got our start—if anything is started—
in the egg chair.
"Sure."

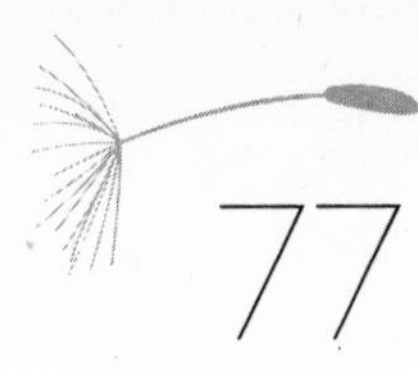

77

"Hey, Goth Girl!" Justine catches up with me
in the parking lot after school,
Ned a few paces behind her.

"Please don't call me that."

"What do you want me to call you?"

Justine's Monday outfit is absent its usual touch of pink.
Instead she wears a crisp white blouse over a pleated
blue mini, very "naughty schoolgirl,"
or perhaps not so naughty
with those three-quarter sleeves
mimicking Ned's "ready to work" effect.

Are we so easily transformed by boys?
So quickly angelified
or darkened
by their attention
or disaffection?

"Just plain Daisy's worked since forever." I try to smile.

Now Dave is sauntering around the side of the school.
Should I keep chatting with Justine?
Fill the time required for him to reach the parking lot?

"I know you've got to go home now," Justine says.
"But wanna come for ice cream with me and Ned
tomorrow after school? You could invite . . ."

"I've gotta do some tutoring."

Ned wraps his hands around Justine's good-girl middle,
his cheek pressing against her flat-ironed hair.
"Tutoring. That's cool," he says.

"What kind?" Justine asks.

"Helping Cal O'Casey with A-PUSH."
And maybe, just maybe, I'm a little glad
to see the lift in her eyebrows, the second's hesitation
before she completes her turn into Ned's arms.

78

I cling to the steering wheel,
trying not to look in my rearview mirror at Dave
reaching his Fiesta's parking spot,
pocketing his phone,
flipping through his ring of keys.

It starts to rain as I pull onto Main Street.
Wishing for the drop of five degrees
that would transform the wet to snow,
I switch on the windshield wipers.
There is never a perfect wiper speed
to smooth away the rain:
Kind of like making out, the fast setting is too fast;
the slow too slow to clear the driver's view of the road
through the falling water.

"Hey, Daisy," Mom calls as I come in the door.

"Hi." I'm puzzled by her jeans and sweater.
"No yoga tonight?"

"No, something different."
Her smile fades into confusion as she takes in my eyes,
my nails.
"You look . . . different, too."

That's when two text lines from Dave
buzz into my phone.
"Why'd you run from the parking lot just now?"

"I'll, uh, be right back.
Just gonna drop my backpack in my room."

Steven's head turns slightly as I double-time it
up the stairs, but even darkened Keds
don't make much noise on hardwood.

I set my bag by the door, which I push carefully shut;
sit on my unmade bed.
Heart pounding, I look at the lines again,
wishing I could call Justine right now, ask her what to do.
I could, I guess, but I know that would mean my story
might be shared with Ned.

Ned Hoffman:
a perfectly decent guy
and the embodiment of all that is frustrating

about small-town life.
Ned Hoffman, who also knows about everyone's sordid
sagas. Though everybody does in Jasper,
not everybody makes you feel like, when they look at you,
all they see are your unsecret secrets.
Ned Hoffman does.
Ned Hoffman, who is now kissing my best friend.

"If you don't text back,
I'm gonna dial this phone and actually call you."
More lines zing from broken-family, stepchild,
make-out-buddy Dave.
Has Ned heard about that yet?

I ransack my memories of HBO romances,
wonder what to type back to Dave,
but no sexy high-fantasy
or teen-about-to-die-falls-in-love story I can recall
suggests the words I should use,
the words that could hold the longing,
the uncertainty in my heart.

That's kind of blue.

79

I nearly throw the phone across the room
when, seconds later, the voice of Yoda
begins insistently repeating,
"Ringing I am; this is your phone calling,"
a ringtone I haven't changed since my
obsession with *Star Wars*
evolved into HBO nights.

I am holding the slim phone like it could burst into flame.
Answer or ignore?
The second option makes me think of a word
I attach so often to Steven—
he is ignoring me . . . I am being ignored—
even though I know it isn't right.

I press the "answer" button,
mute with uncertainty.

"Daisy? You there? You okay?"
Dave's voice is rumbly-warm,
concerned,

a little sexy.
Not ignoring me.
The opposite of that.

"Yeah. I'm here."

"So, you gonna tell me what happened
back at the parking lot?
Were you running away?"

"Shouldn't I run"—
I try to make my voice sound teasing—
"from a bad boy like you?"

Now it's my turn to listen to silence.
Moment follows moment, filled only with the sound
of blood swishing in my pressed-to-phone ear.

"I'm not bad," Dave says at last. "There's no such thing."
"There are only boys
and girls
and good and bad situations."

My heart reaches out to his words.

Is Steven bad?

Dangerous, certainly.
But will I ever know for certain
what his motives, morals are?
Does he?
Did my parents commit some evil to deserve this?
Did I?

As if I believed in such supernatural things,
as if I hadn't trodden this ground a thousand times
in counseling sessions, been reassured
by nodding, liberal PhDs
with normal children.
How can they know?
They are not any smarter than my parents, than me.
I shake my mind from this dangerous path.

"Bad situations," I begin my reply. "Like what to do
after you kiss a not-bad-boy in the dark by the pits."

"I should've called before now, but—" Dave pauses.
I imagine him flicking his lighter,
spinning a beer cap between his finger and thumb.
"Hell, Daisy, even though we haven't really hung out
in years, we've known each other
since before we could tie our own shoes.
It just felt . . .

I kind of don't know what happened Saturday night."

"Me either."

"So now what?" he asks.

His question means that he doesn't want nothing.
If he'd wanted nothing, he could have just pretended
not to see me speed away from school.
His question has begun an improvisation between us,
a call-and-response.
It's my turn to pick up the melody, take responsibility
for our direction.
I imagine my trumpet in my hands, long for a sound,
a sentence, beautiful and clear.
Inhale.
What I think I want
is a dozen more nights of chilly lakeside kisses
without reflection or remorse.
What I say is,
"Meet up in the library tomorrow after school?"

"You. Me. The egg chair." Dave's voice sounds glad.
"I'll bring the music."

80

"Dinnertime, Daisy!"
Mom's voice rises up, loud enough for me to hear
but in one of her practiced, modulated,
keep-the-peace tones.

As usual, I start down the stairs without calling back.
Don't want to start a dialogue that might sound like
yelling,
might turn the night sour for Steven,
for us all.

"Sheila will be here soon,"
Mom says as she passes me a plate of leftovers,
her eyes bright as if she is offering candy.
Steven is already working on his slightly cooled
grilled cheese sandwich.
"Dad can meet us at the movie theater.
Thought maybe we'd catch the new Bond
and then go for ice cream."

Sheila is what is known as a "respite caregiver,"
a glorified, qualified, brave babysitter who, for a price,

lets family members escape their eternal roles as
therapists, doctors, nurses,
slaves
to the disabled yet powerful rulers of their lives.

When you've been on the autism hamster wheel
long enough,
and if you have the cash,
you've paid for one sometime along the way.

Once Dad said the worst socioeconomic bracket
to be autistic in
was the middle class.
Yeah, we have granite countertops and a two-car garage.
We could theoretically take spring break trips to
warm places, Disney World.
I own a very nice, way-above-student-grade Bach trumpet.
But there is no budget, no program, no viable plan
to help us navigate through Steven's world.
Just pamphlets,
"advice" to "make him part of our community"
and "foster understanding,"
admonishments about taking care of ourselves
along with our "special-needs family member";
community groups laden with others like us,
trying not to complain—to cry;

education plans hard-won from cost-conscious,
understaffed public schools
who have had no more luck teaching Steven
to button and tie than my mother.

81

"Cool" is my one-word answer,
deep with the worry that Steven will hurt Sheila,
resonant with doubt that Dad will actually show up,
scoffing at the implication that a movie and ice cream
are part of any solution.

Mom raises one finely tweezed eyebrow, says nothing.
I push the food around my plate,
from the corner of my eye watch Steven bite, chew,
swallow.

Mom is quick to the door when the bell rings.
Sheila, fattish, slugs out of her gray wool coat,
tucks her scarf into one sleeve.
"Now, where's my friend Steven?" she asks.

Mom smiles, leads the way.
"Remember, Steven, tonight we're going to have fun
with our friend Sheila.
She's going to play Blokus with you.
Here, Sheila, I have Steven's game ready."

"I remember Steven."
Sheila continues Mom's simple, steady cadence.
For the uninitiated, this is a technique called
"social stories"—a strategy used with autistic kids
to help model what a routine
or change in routine will be like.
There are even "social stories" books on how
to ride a bus or go to the store.
"I like Blokus, too, Steven. Let's play Blokus together."
Sheila lowers her wide ass onto the kitchen chair
beside Steven.

I feel an inexplicable wave of hatred shimmer through me,
wanting to scream "farce, farce" into this tragic display,
then remembering how much I wished
someone would give me lines
to say to Dave,
wondering if "social stories" could be written
to guide geekoid trumpet girls, too.

"And then"—lifting her tone brightly,
Mom catches Sheila's eye,
points to two plates by the sink—
"you can have cookies."

Sounds like we're fattening him, doesn't it?

Like we ply him with cookies to buy his acquiescence?
Those cookies are laden with wheat germ and flaxseed oil,
all kinds of things to help Steven's unruly gut.
He is chubby from all his meds,
but it's not like anyone can force him to exercise
like we used to when he was smaller.
Dad kept trying to take him on weekend runs
even after he started turning off the route,
coursing toward the middle of streets
without regard for the rules and dangers of traffic.
The runs finally ended with Steven's first pimple,
the first extra shower he had to take
because he stank of sweat.

"And Daisy and Dad and I will be home in no time,"
Mom finishes sweetly.

"See you later, Steven and Sheila."
I follow Mom to the front hall.

Her eyes sparkle as she hands me my jacket.
"I can't remember the last time
I saw a first-run movie in a theater."

Neither one of us follows through to the evil endpoint
of this thought:

that when Steven moves away we can do this anytime.

"I thought, maybe, you had gone to see James Bond,
that maybe that's where you were last night."
Her voice is tentative,
as if she didn't have a right to ask where I was
or to be angry at me.

But I want her to be angry
and toast my waffles
and say things that Shirley says to Justine—
"you're only seventeen"—and not just tell me
I'm late and then shut her mouth, or rush off to yoga
and not ask if I "approve" of huge decisions.
I want her to tell me something is better—or worse—
not merely "best for the family";
to tell me how she *feels* about things.

Somehow, somewhere along the way,
all the autism experts' plans
outlining how to model social interaction,
appropriate behavior, life skills for Steven, flip-flopped,
and instead
my brother has taught the rest of us
to never show what we feel.

Maybe not to feel at all.

But right now I do feel angry.
Right now I want
to dive into Mom's arms and tell her I've been kissed—
really kissed—
and that I've tasted beer and felt my heart skip
and am worried because I don't know
if Justine's boyfriend is right for her,
and I don't know if Dave is mine . . .

But "I hear it's a good one," is how I answer my mother.

Dad meets us at the movie theater entrance,
wallet already open,
and buys us three movie tickets.

As Mom says to Dad,
"Daisy tells me this should be good,"
Dave's words echo back to me:
There are no bad or good people,
only girls and boys
and good and bad situations.

82

"I don't know if there's time for ice cream,"
Dad says as we walk back to the car.
"And Daisy was out late last night."

"Ted." Mom tucks her hand in the bend of his elbow.
"We agreed to trust."

"I kind of do feel like ice cream," I say.
I want to be as contrary as my kohl-ringed eyes,
which they refuse to comment on.
And, angry as I am, some part of me also wants
the smile on Mom's lips,
the interlacing of my parents' arms
to last as long as possible.

"Okay, takeout," Dad says,
glancing only once at his watch.
I am rewarded by Mom's girlish giggle
as vanilla drips over the edge of her cone
onto the sleeve of her faux fur coat.
Dad grins as he dabs at it with a paper napkin.

I sit in the rear of the car on the way home,
watching the backs of my parents' heads
tilt slightly toward each other in the front seats.
Tell myself to trust,
maybe forgive them
just a little.

83

It is not until I see Cal
in jazz band on Tuesday morning
that I realize I've booked myself an awkward afternoon:
a three o'clock Dave-and-Cal-and-me library triangle
that certainly won't fit into the oval egg chair.

I slide the mouthpiece onto my trumpet,
wishing I'd realized this soon enough to call Justine
and get some advice on unraveling the mess I've made.
But no, I am on my own,
trapped between Cal's quick grin
and the back of Dave's messy-perfect head
leaning against the band room window.

84

Time always goes too fast in jazz band.
Today is no exception.
We wrap with a swing medley of Christmas tunes
I usually enjoy,
though I pretty well trash my feature in "I'll Be Home for Christmas,"
rushing through like a squawking beginner.
I am trembling from my lips to my toes.

Cal is careful packing up his instrument,
so it's easy to shove my trumpet case on the shelf,
escape the band room before he has the chance to talk to me.

Dave is smiling, eyes closed, earbuds in,
listening to a tune, softly mouthing the words
as though this hall were empty
of the throngs of hair-swinging,
style-judging, ball-tossing,
book-worming high schoolers.

Hey, la-la. It's gonna be okay today.
Hey, hi-hi. It's gonna be all right tonight.

I recognize the refrain.
It's a song by one of those folksy rock groups
whose name is some random combination
of nonprimary color and funky notion:
Black Rainbow,
Gray Fantasy,
Shining Obsolescence.

Not unlike the Irish ballads
Dad used to sing for my lullabies:
The lyrics are a mixture of anger and reassurance,
hurt and heart,
and if they have no conclusion,
they just fade the tune away.

I envy rock musicians' escape into refrains,
into mantras of easy words
to validate their drumbeats and oft-simple melodies.

Sometimes, it seems to me that lyrics turn pure sound
to lies—
the words forced to fit music that says so much more
when left
unexplained.

I tap Dave's shoulder.
He doesn't startle as he opens his eyes,
takes in my made-up face,
my somber sweater and jeans.
"Hey there, Daisy-brains. You're looking dark today."

"I can't meet you in the library this afternoon.
I mean, I'll be there,
but I'm supposed to do some tutoring and . . ."
My tumble-rush of an excuse
for something that's really perfectly innocent
comes with the heat of a rising blush
that turns my shivers to sweat.

"It's okay," he says, grabbing my damp hand.
"How about we pick up again Saturday night,
back at the lake?"

I nod.
It's that easy.

"Catch ya at lunchtime, too, maybe."
Dave pushes away from the wall,
slides his hand behind my neck,
brushes his mouth against mine just as Cal comes out
of the band room.

I see the Irish edges of his upturned lips go straight.
He turns the opposite way from Dave and me.

Never that easy.

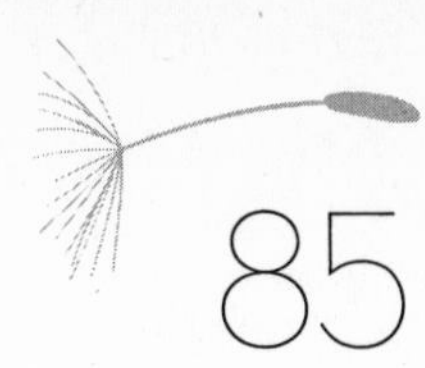

85

In A-PUSH, Justine passes me a folded magazine page.
A model poses in torn black tights and a plaid pinafore.
"Goth and Prepster meet in the middle?"
is scrawled in Sharpie across the top.

I turn from Mr. Angelli's unemotional recounting
of the horrendously bloody Battle of Antietam
to give her a giant smile.
Justine—my best friend—child of divorce,
expert in compromise,
all-around hilarious girl.
If she likes Ned, I've got to give him a chance.
I know she's already doing the same for me and Dave
even without my asking,
even without my knowing
what "me and Dave" really means.

"Dave asked me out for Saturday night," I whisper.

A squeak emerges from Justine,
loud enough to draw Mr. Angelli's attention.

But he just shrugs and returns to his map.
"Your AP scores will not be enhanced
by gossiping during class." The Angelli-style reprimand
is delivered in the same dry tone
he uses to detail gruesome Civil War atrocities.
His eyes don't flare with Mrs. Pendleton's irritation,
passion, which I don't like but I get.
For a second I try to imagine a Mrs. Angelli—
I've heard there is one—
but all I can picture
is a woman in a long brown prairie dress and bonnet
chastely reading history books;
nothing HBO at all.

Justine waggles her finger, murmurs,
"Will *not* be enhanced,"
and we shake with silent giggles.

"Where are you and Dave going?" Justine asks.

"To . . ." I don't want to say the pits.
I have asked Dave for very little and now I see
he's given me exactly that:
a chance to lock lips again underneath a chill sky.
Maybe I want Dave to pick me up at the door,
take me to a meal, ask me to a dance.

"We're working on a plan," is all I can think to say.

"La Parisienne was awesome," she replies lightly.

I'm certain there's no way Dave could afford such a tab.
Since his folks broke up, he's lived in the older part of town
where seventies split-levels pepper squat lots
with postage-stamp backyards too small for swing sets
and sandboxes.

I think of Cal's holey jeans,
Steven's high-priced tracksuits,
Shirley's extravagantly feminine bathroom.
How many La Parisienne dinners would it take
to match the price
of a year of residential care for my brother?
How many elegant pink prom dresses
might buy a daughter's forgiveness
for a father who left his only child?

I wonder if Justine knows her restaurant suggestion
is out of Dave's reach
but needs, despite her love for me, to twist a knife,
prove there's a guy out there who wants
to spend time with her.

I don't like the way boys have driven
little wedges into our friendship, pushed Justine and me
to instances where we treat each other
with Ashleigh Anderson–style unkindness.
Maybe, though, this is one of those times
that I should use my talent for quiet,
for acceptance—
let my best friend have her moment
to flounce her pleated skirt and walk away.

86

"He your boyfriend?"
are Cal's first words to me in the library.

"Who?" I reply dumbly as if I don't know,
buying time to think of the answer I don't have.

"That Dave fella."

His gaze is clear, his lips set straight.
He is holding a spiral-bound notebook in his right hand.
A pencil is tucked behind his ear.

"I don't know. You wanna get started on some history?"
I walk toward the row of private study rooms at the back
of the library.
Cal follows me.

87

Cal sets biographies
of Harriet Tubman and Frederick Douglass,
Harriet Beecher Stowe's *Uncle Tom's Cabin*,
and half a dozen other books
on the study room table.

I look at the names, the titles on the covers,
all familiar to me, people and stories
about which I have been taught since grade school,
but books I have never read.
"Have you read all these?"

"Some. Others, just pages here and there.
I am wonderin' if we should try writin' about a lad
or a lass,
someone stuck on a Southern plantation
or someone who's made it on that Railroad to freedom."

There's something about the way his voice breaks
on that word, *freedom*,
that makes me look up from *When I Was a Slave*

with its frightening cover illustration of a bleak-faced family
standing before an endless field of cotton.

I picture Cal, alone, on an airplane from Ireland;
imagine slave children being sold from their parents,
shipped away to other plantations,
to strange, unfamiliar worlds.
When I look back down, the faces on the book's cover
have all turned to Steven's.

"Let's make it a boy."
My voice struggles for its don't-pity-me tone;
my lips tighten
as if I'm about to buzz a high C on my trumpet.
Even after I'm able to swallow,
my eyes feel embarrassingly wet.
"And let's make him . . . free."

"Right then," Cal replies softly.
He sits down in one of the wooden chairs.
I sit down, too.

The dusty library air is electric with secrets
almost palpable in the thick quiet that bounces between
Cal and those books and me.

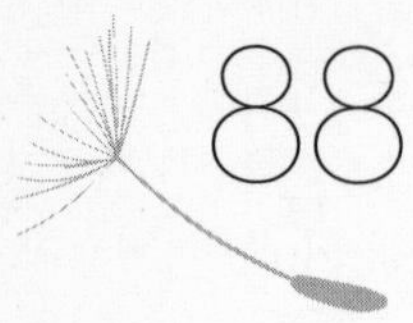

88

Two hours later, I am driving home
unprompted by a text from Mom,
my stomach growling despite an A-plus hot lunch
of oven-fried chicken legs and fruit salad.

Cal and I have named our freed slave Jeremy—
his idea,
and I don't ask the reason.
We've given him a home in Pennsylvania,
the first of the United States to pass an Abolition Act—
that idea was mine.

E-mail and cell numbers written down.
Research for Jeremy's backstory, family tree,
current living conditions, divided.
Plans made to meet again on Thursday.
All painfully established between the arcs of silence,
the epic string of whole rests
that scored our time in the study room.
We're both horn players, well trained to wait
through swathes of music

featuring flutes and clarinets and strings,
obedient in a certain way.

Despite my love of jazz, I failed at improvisation here.

My stomach churns again,
a wave of nauseous despair battling hungry acid.
Neither of us touched the last question
on the A-PUSH assignment rubric;
neither of us dared to invent
Jeremy's future dreams.

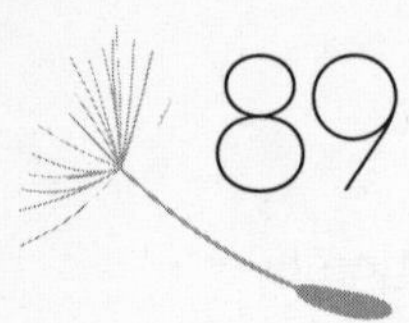

89

Wednesday morning
Mom leaves Steven's waffle too long in the toaster.
I freeze at my post at the island,
knowing too well what may happen
when the charred smell of burnt Eggo
reaches my brother's nose.

Steven's head whips straight back,
making contact with the kitchen wall behind his chair.
A pause, another whack. Then his elbows close in,
the hand-wringing begins.
The masochistic scraping of his palms is more bearable
than the *bam* of his skull
hitting the already-weakened drywall.
But the smell is too much for just writhing.
Smack! Head slams back again.
Hands twist sixty seconds more.
Smack!

Mom hovers indecisively between the toaster
and the table, watching the writhing,

hoping Steven will spare his skull
long enough for her to clean up the mess.
Finally, "Be right back."
She pinches the smoking disk
between surely-singeing forefinger and thumb,
runs to toss it out the door.

"Morning, everybody." Dad saunters into the kitchen,
adjusting his tie, gearing up for our routines.
He scans the room for Mom only to find her, wild-eyed,
returning from the hall.
Sees the statue of me at the island.
Hears a nasal sound emerge from Steven. Then silence.

Smack!

Above Steven's head,
a narrow fissure appears
in the putty-colored paint.

"I-I burnt the waffle," Mom whispers.

A curtain drops over Dad's eyes.
His expression becomes a replica of a human's,
like that of a bust of Haydn;
he morphs into "brave robot," "man of the family,"

the only one big enough to move toward Steven,
even though it's an action not unlike
bashing one's own head against a wall:
a promise of pain.

"Morning, Steven."
He approaches the kitchen table slowly.
An unconvincing smile cracks the plaster of his face.
"Your waffle will be ready soon.
Then we'll take our ride to school, won't we?
Because today is a school day."

He is rewarded with a flashing fist,
a punch into the soft part of his side, below his ribs.
He grabs Steven's forearm. "No, Steven.
That's not what we do, Steven."

My brother makes few sounds as he struggles and lashes,
the snap of his head connecting with the wall
one last time
before Dad drags him from his chair,
through the doorway to the hall.
I can't help myself. I rise from my chair,
watch them pass Mom, cowering against the fridge.
In his stocking-feet, Steven half-slides
toward the living room.

“God dammit,” Dad shouts to no one in particular.

“I don’t know what to do.”

90

All things eventually end, don't they?
Minutes, hours, days;
songs, stories;
lives as we know them.

By the time the outburst has ended,
there's a patch of sticky, blood-matted hair
on the back of Steven's head,
but Mom is afraid to get close enough to check the cut
that surely lies beneath it.
Dad returns him to his kitchen chair.
Steven eats the new waffle Mom has successfully toasted.

"Want me to come with you to the ER?" Mom asks.

"You don't think the nurse can just check this at school?"
Dad adjusts his tie.

"They might need to x-ray . . ."
She's crying now, very softly.
We continue each step in our routine,

just later than usual.
Trying not to quicken the pace, invite another punch.

This morning is another nail
in the coffin of my parents' decision.
Without details, without a timeline, still I realize
that the *eventually* with which this family will be broken apart
is going to come soon.

My days watching Mom and Dad and Steven
around the kitchen table are numbered.

The house grows still, the only sounds
Steven's slightly stuffy breathing,
the occasional *tink* of his fork against the waffle plate.

I try to feel love for him
but come up with only a heart full of confusion
and a yearning not to break this gentle silence
by pushing back my barstool,
snapping shut my horn case,
rifling through my key ring.

So I cannot leave for jazz band.

My father walks slowly around the table,
looks at Steven's head. "Can't be too bad.
Heads bleed like crazy, and this has already stopped
without our even touching it.
I'm bringing him to school."

I hate the victory in Dad's expression.

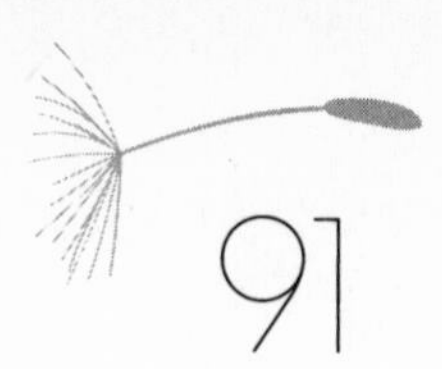

91

"Love you, Steven," Mom musters
as we watch Dad usher him belatedly out the door.

I don't know what meaning she feels behind that word.
Whom do we love, anyway?
People who love us?
People who care for us?
People who are put in our care?

Is love trust, understanding,
the ability to communicate?
Is it the ability to touch
and be touched in return?

Is it the humble ritual of bending to tie sneakers,
of returning from the office,
albeit late and with grim reluctance,
to give a boy a shower?

I don't think I know anymore
what the meaning of that word is

or how to find it
or how to give it up.

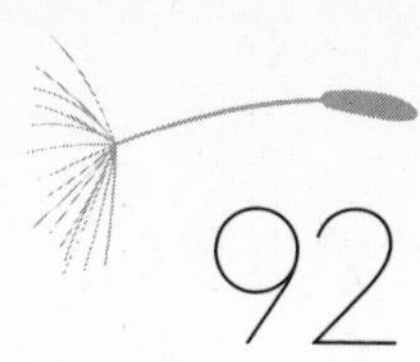

92

Thursday morning, it is easier not to go to practice.
I leave the house as if jazz band were my destination,
but I cannot bear the thought of the squawks and
squeals of tuning up,
the cheer of chatter among musicians.

My blue varnished fingers clutch the steering wheel.
I remember the rebellious wet,
the gratifying cold of applying polish.
But darkened eyes and nails are not enough
to make my parents realize that this decision for Steven
must be theirs, not mine.
That if (or when) he is gone, I may never be able to feel
safety without sorrow,
relief without remorse.

It is hard to be a rebel with good grades
and a three-year All-State number one trumpeter streak.

I love making honor roll. I love playing beautiful sounds
that make people forget

all they know about my difficult daily life,
about the bad parts of the days they endured before they
opened up their ears.
But if I keep playing, how can I show Jasper
there's a tragedy happening in its midst
without actually telling anyone?

I drive to Evergreen High,
park in a spot far away from the door,
curl up like a kitten in the driver's seat,
leave the motor running to keep the car warm.

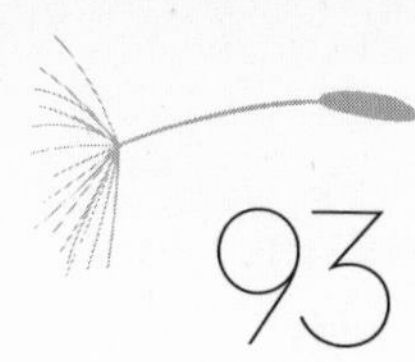

93

"I've been learnin' about your American Thanksgiving,"
Cal greets me in the library after school.
"It was Abe Lincoln there who proclaimed it
a national holiday, to try to get a sense of unity
'tween the North and the South."

"Aren't *you* the studious one." I don't tell him
I'd assumed Thanksgiving was a steady date
from the days of feathered headdresses
and square-buckled pilgrim hats.
Lincoln was Gettysburg, the ironclad USS *Monitor*,
assassination,
not turkey and gravy.
"What's that got to do with our slave?"

"I was thinkin' about how our lad
might spend his first free Thanksgiving,
but the research tells me it'd probably be the same
kind o' day as any other."

He looks disappointed by the notion,

as if it cannot be the case
that this grand American holiday
might have passed unnoticed by so many citizens.
But I am unsurprised by the notion
of extraordinary days performed as ordinary:
the narrative of my life.
I rub the inside corners of my eyes with my middle
finger and thumb.
"Writing stories is harder than playing music, isn't it?
Weaving together all these facts is not the same
as playing a score."

"Life is a big story. Music is just one way to tell it,
to realize how many tales all kinds of people share.
Like this North and South; we've got that in Ireland, too.
'The Troubles,' they call that history.
All about religious freedom,
Home Rule."

"We've got a slew of rules at home." I laugh, then
my automatic instinct to keep my family's front door closed
kicks in. I glare into the curiosity sparking in Cal's eyes.
"Race or religion, people are always battling
on one kind of moral ground or another. The question
is whether we should start this story on Thanksgiving Day."

Cal looks thoughtful.
"So, would Jeremy know it was Thanksgiving?
Who would tell him?
And would we want this to be the day he was freed?"

I can't help but smile at his energy, his effort.
It makes me want to say I'm sorry
for not wanting to share Aggie with him,
for not caring enough about this fiction we are making.
"You got stuck with a crap history tutor, Cal," I tell him.

"But a damn fine musician.
Even if you don't show up for jazz band two days running."

94

I know that somewhere
in Mom's laundry list of unread e-mails
is one from the Evergreen High attendance office
(and maybe one from Mr. Orson, too),
noting my two days of unexcused absences
from zero-period jazz band.

I should feel guilty about this,
like I feel guilty about letting poor Irish Cal
do way more than half the work for our A-PUSH project,
about still not having chosen a solo
for the holiday band concert.
I should feel afraid for the possible consequences, but
they shrivel in the wake of Dad's after-dinner proclamation:
"This weekend, we're all going to visit Holland House,
a special school—a home—for kids like Steven."

A hunger for Dave's careless grin
is the only feeling in my stomach,
as I think I'll skip jazz band again tomorrow.

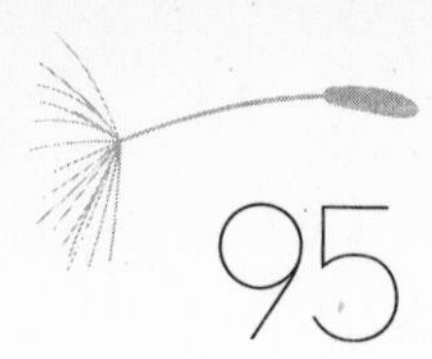

95

Friday morning, Mom begins feeding my brother
a steady diet of
"Tomorrow, we are going to take a drive.
Tomorrow, we are going to visit a fun place.
We will visit for a little while,
then come right home and have lunch,"
along with the symmetrical waffles
and tepid mac and cheese.

I almost forget to pick up Justine, whose car is in the shop,
on the way to school.
"Thanks for the lift." She wafts into the passenger seat
on a wave of gardenia.

The first inhale is pleasure, but the second, third,
turn the scent cloying.
Justine grins as she watches my nose crinkle.
"It's Calvin Klein. Mom brought home a sample from work.
Forgot your thing about smells."

"No." I try to unfurrow my brow. "I like it."

"Ned does." She giggles.
"He says it makes my neck smell delicious."

"He says that? Ew!" I squeal. But now I'm smiling,
even though Justine has flooded my car
with an overpowering stink of flowers.
I pull onto Main Street,
finally finding a bit of sorrow in my numb heart
for the way our lives,
which used to revolve so much around each other,
have begun to drift into strange new orbits
polluted with scents and boys
and secrets.
Well, my secrets.

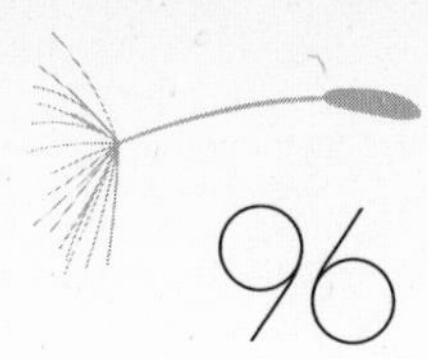

96

The high school parking lot is close to empty
at this early hour. Still, I pull into a spot far from
the building.

"Daisy, do you really need me to walk a mile in these
heels?" She wiggles her stilettoed feet, sighs.
"I do like how Ned is so tall."

I flash to a memory of Justine,
dressed in high ten-year-old style,
down to her sparkle-toed half-inch heels,
standing between my parents
outside the artists' exit of a concert hall.
(Shirley was at our house watching Steven,
still a manageably small, silent little boy
who would passively push cars across the floor for hours,
whose ticks and stims had not begun to destroy walls,
draw blood.)

It was my first time playing a solo
with the state orchestra, so, of course,
she'd come to listen.

I've never liked remembering that day,
its highlight feature being the mistake I made
just a few notes in.
Aggie had told me a zillion times,
"Don't worry if you hit a bad note;
just put it behind you and play the next one.
Keep moving forward through the music."
But the instant I heard that absurdly awful E-flat escape
my instrument, everything I knew about the trumpet
floated with it, out into the cavernous auditorium.
I could almost see notes, technique, counts
as sparkles of dust skittering
along the beams of stage light
away from my grasp.

I dissolved into four beats of silence,
redeemed only by the conductor's hang-in-there smile,
his "and ah-one, two," the encouraging lilt of his baton
that brought me back to the music.
After, I bowed at the audience's polite applause,
did not break again until I was back in the greenroom,
awash in confused humiliation.
How could I, the prodigy,
the sister-of-the-living-mistake
who never made them herself,

fall so far from my pedestal so fast?

Now, the memory shifts,
the sting of the false note fading, replaced by the image
of Justine's thousand-watt grin shining
from between my parents' uncertain half-smiles:
"You looked amazing in that blue dress!"

"But I . . . but I . . ."
Even then, words had a habit of failing me.

"What, you missed a note? Nobody noticed."

"You did."

"No, I didn't. You are amazing and I dare anyone
to say different." Her eyes as defiant
as they were the morning of Cal O'Casey's homeroom snub,
her preteen back straight,
balancing perfectly on her heels.
"Let's go get ice cream."

97

"What's the matter, Daisy?" Justine asks me now.
"You look so upset."
"Were you right? Are your parents splitting up?"

I shake my head. "No."

"Then what is it?"

I am hungry to tell her, to ask her what to do,
but I choke on the words, afraid
that Justine might finally fail to make me laugh—
be unable to piece the shattered mess of me
back together.
And then where will I turn?
"It's . . . hard to talk about."

"Are you in trouble?"
Justine's question is so quick,
her implied worry so obvious,
that I wonder if she, too, is keeping secrets,
if what she's doing with her new boyfriend

is maybe more than I imagined it could be.

"Nothing like that.
It's just that life has gotten so confusing lately.
I feel like everyone wants me to agree to things
I don't even want to think about."

Justine, puzzled, looks at her watch.
"You're late for jazz band."

"It's okay."

"You've never said that before."
She squeezes my right shoulder.
"You're my best friend, Daisy.
When you're ready to talk, I'll listen."

She opens the car door,
plants her stylish shoes on the frost-covered pavement,
and gives me a friendly wave.
Her back is straight, her walk eternally confident.
As if on cue, Ned's car pulls in. He drives up alongside her.
Justine's bright laugh echoes across the parking lot
as she gets in and is chauffeured
to the closest row of spots after all.

98

What am I doing, sitting in this parking lot,
listening to raindrops pelt the roof of my car,
not playing my trumpet?

A tap on my window.
I roll it down for Dave.
"Aren't you supposed to be in jazz band, Daisy-brains?"

"Is that all anyone wants to know?"

"Well, whatcha sitting here for?"

"I have a headache," my stupid mouth answers.
I sound frighteningly like my mother.

Dave goes round to the passenger side of the car. Gets in.

I turn on the CD player.
Ella Fitzgerald's unmistakable voice
eases into "Body and Soul,"
holding on to each note like it tastes good in her mouth.

"Thought you said you had a headache."
Dave gives a lock of my brown hair a little tug.

"Not that kind," I answer, as if that means something,
blushing at thoughts of the Dave-and-me fantasies
I've dreamed to this track.

"What kind, then?"

"The kind that makes me want to have a little 'relax'
out here in my car."

"Maybe it's from all the dark eye makeup," he says.

"Do you have a problem with my eyes?"
I ball my fist.

"Hey, hey, no. It's a cool look; it just . . .
doesn't seem *you*, y'know?"

"People can change," I snap.

"I guess we've both changed."
He scrapes his fingers through his hair.

"Change . . ." I let my hands relax.
Feel the fragility of the word as it sighs through my lips,
like *sorry*, its meaning easily worn away by overuse,
from a start that's vague already;
as easily for the bad as for the good.
". . . is scary."

"It's the story of life." Dave puts his hand on top of mine,
rubs away the lingering traces of fist,
sending shivers of want up my spine.

"Then life is kind of a horror film." I try to smile.

"Wanna go to The Movie House tonight?"
He tilts the seat back so he can look out the car's skylight.
"We're going to see the new Bond."

"I already saw it with my parents."
The words sound lame the second they leave my lips.
Worse than lame:
I-just-turned-down-a-real-date-with-Dave-Miller stupid.
"Besides, I have to babysit, er, hang out with Steven."

He shrugs.
"I never let the twinlets interfere with my plans."

"That's different.
Your stepmom can just get a regular sitter.
We can't anymore."

"Yeah, I heard."
Unlike super-citizen Ned,
Dave doesn't pretend he hasn't heard the gossip,
the story told by the neighbor lady
who was watching Steven the afternoon
of the Great Closet Door Kick-In Incident.
"Still, your parents kind of own your time."

"I know. I wish I could go to the movies tonight. I just . . ."

His eyes lock on to mine;
fringed by thick black lashes,
those knee-jellifying, brown-flecked-with-yellow irises
meet my basic blues.
"I get it."

He puts his hand behind my neck
in a way that's starting to feel familiar.
A morning kiss, firm, tantalizing.
I lean forward, my elbow grazing the horn.
We are pulled apart by the sharp honk.

"Oops."

"Very romantic," he teases.
He is smiling, straightening the rumple
he's made of my hair,
even though he never fixes his own.
"How 'bout I pick you up tomorrow at your house?
Seven-ish?"

"I'll be ready." Another lame reply.

He gets out of my car, saunters toward the school,
and I am watching him walk away again,
replaying my stupid words, wishing
that tonight I'd be going to watch James Bond
once again save the world
instead of laying out Blokus pieces,
even though I know it may be one of the last weeks
I'll be living in a prison of boredom and frustration
and a little bit of fear.

Why can't I be as casual about Steven
as Dave is about the twinlets?
Or maybe he isn't.
Maybe he, like me,
is engaged in the kind of unspoken rebellion

you don't want to perform too brightly,
since you're never certain
anyone in your family will notice
your darkened eyes, skeleton shoes, tousled hair,
patchy attendance record.
You may be sacrificing body and soul
on a ghostly battlefield, fighting across a divide
seen by no one
but you.

99

"Wanna get Thai after orchestra tomorrow?"
Justine asks me at lunch.

"I can't go to orchestra. Family plans."

"You never have family plans.
Now you've *got* to tell me what's up!"

"It's a secret. Promise not to tell Ned?" I whisper.

Justine almost puts on her
you-can't-believe-how-scary-these-freckles-can-be
expression, the one she uses
when a freshman hogs the bathroom mirror
or Ashleigh Anderson calls us "you girls."

"Please, Jussie?"
I haven't called her that since we were in third grade,
when she decided she wanted to have a nickname
like mine
even though I'd pointed out that

Justine was a cool name and, really,
there was no time for me to write out Margaret-Mary
on every spelling test.
Still, we were Daisy and Jussie for most of the year,
even though she is *so* a Justine:
clever, sharp-witted,
and compassionate in her oh-so-feisty way.

Her scary-freckle-face subsides.
"Okay, Margaret-Mary."

"My parents are going to put Steven in an institution."

And the words are out,
like school cafeteria mashed potatoes
slopped onto a lunch tray,
congealing under gray-white gravy,
ugly and cold.

"Oh my God." Her voice is hushed.
And I know she won't tell Ned,
despite being chronically glued to his side.
Honestly, I am happy for her, even a little jealous,
and so, so lonely.

100

"Hey, babe."

It's Ned, of course.
Justine slides over
to make room for him on the bench beside her.
"We were just talking about you," she says.
"How I love that you're so tall, so I can wear high heels."
Her comment is adorable,
her lie seamless.

"They look amazing."
Ned wraps his thin arm around her shoulders.

"I could never stand in shoes like that,"
I say, finding my tongue.

"Sneakers totally suit you," Justine says.

I look down at today's Keds.
Despite my recent attempts at Gothdom, somehow,
today, an old pair sporting kelly-green shamrock stamps
and rainbow laces

has found its way onto my feet.

"Erin go bragh!" Ned laughs.

It's a Gaelic phrase, meaning "Ireland forever."
Quite senseless in this context,
but I am used to nonsense words
and, unburdened from my Steven secret,
feeling strangely light.

"You know that makes no sense, Ned," I say.

"I don't even know what it means," Ned says.
"Just, your shoes make me think of Saint Patrick's Day."

"You're way too tall to be a leprechaun." Justine giggles.

In the corner of my eye,
I see true Irish Cal O'Casey
sitting on the fringes
of the bookworm crowd at a table nearby,
his long legs stretching into the lunchroom's center aisle.

I think he's even taller than Ned.

101

No yoga for Mom tonight.
No working late for Dad.
We're a foursome around the kitchen table,
eating mac and cheese
as if it's our last meal before execution
instead of dinner
the night before a two-hour morning drive.

With the exception of her reluctant stoop to Eggo waffles,
Mom makes almost all our food from scratch.
Tonight, each bite tastes of her carefully chosen
whole-grain elbow macaroni,
hand-shredded blend of cheddar and mozzarella.
There's a bright green salad punctuated
by cheery cherry tomatoes.
Water fills the sturdy yet stylish acrylic glasses.

"This is delicious," Dad says.

"Yeah." I nod.

"I worry the food won't be as healthy at . . ."
Mom tries to smile.

We all look to Steven, who says nothing,
just keeps working his spoon through the noodles.
He gets agitated more easily at night,
so Mom avoids giving him a knife or fork.

Dad wipes his mouth on a napkin.
"Don't go to bed too late, Daisy.
We're going to head out around seven in the morning."

"It should be a nice drive," Mom says.
She stands up to clear;
I notice her plate is still nearly full.

Dad gets up, too,
walks over to the sink,
puts his hands on Mom's taut shoulders,
tries to rub her neck,
but she shrugs him off.

I can't watch him try again.
I turn to Steven, still gulping spoonfuls
of his guiltily generous serving of mac and cheese.

"Steven?" I say softly.

He doesn't look up.

"Steven," I say again,
checking quickly to see that my parents aren't watching.

His focus remains on his food,
but I have to try.
"Steven. Do you want to go to a new school?
Do you understand?"

I slide my hand across the table.
He starts at the touch of my fingers to his wrist
and I wonder if I am about to have to recite
another litany of "sorrys" to my parents.
But it's okay; he settles again,
back to dinner.

"We've been through this a thousand times, Alice."
Dad sounds exasperated as he stalks back to the table,
picks up the salad bowl to clear it.
"How much macaroni did you give him?
He's still eating."

102

The noise upstairs rises as Dad showers Steven;
Mom wants the people at Holland House
to see how clean, how nicely dressed we keep him.

In the basement, I play through all the jazz carols
I've missed practicing,
plus Ellington's "Almost Cried."

I don't answer Justine's "good luck tomorrow" text
or read the assigned pages for A-PUSH.
I don't want to go upstairs,
to hear the horrible sounds—
sounds I admit in my heart I'll be relieved not
to have to hear much longer.
I don't want the night to pass, the morning to come.
I want time to stand still,
like the first time Dave kissed me,
in the chill by the lake.
I don't want Christmas to come,
don't want to hear applause for playing some happy
holiday tune.

That's when I realize what solo to play:
Leonard Cohen's "Hallelujah."
Chords blending beauty with grief,
words of loss and praise.

I pull the sheet music from a drawer,
raise my trumpet, knowing the sound will be stopped
at my practice room door,
wishing my parents were listening,
hearing the lyrics in my head
as the notes flow through my horn.
I play it twice through;
my lips burning, I improv on the melody,
reaching, soaring into high notes.
Then I can't do it anymore. I drop into a perfect,
quarter-note-covered listening chair
and pepper it with my tears.

103

The touch of Mom's cool hand on my forearm awakens me.
"Hey, Daisy, time to go up to bed.
We've got to make an early start tomorrow."

"But I haven't finished practicing."
I rub my eyes, muster a shard of consciousness,
remember where I am,
grab my trumpet again.

Mom sits down in the other chair.
"Play something for me, then." She smiles.

It's been so long since I've seen her sitting there.
I don't hold it against my parents.
It's like that story I once heard of a poor family
who, in despair, called the police
on their knife-wielding autistic teen son.
Instead of taking him away, Social Services
whisked the two younger boys from their beds
and put them in foster care,
leaving the bereft parents to manage their eldest,
their volatile home life.

A quicker, cheaper solution
than finding another place for a dangerous, nonverbal
man-child.

You hear stories like that.

There is a point you reach
where there's no real help, only indentured servitude.
Parents dominated by a child-master who hits, shrieks,
smashes,
while they quiver beneath
the umbrella of family-preserving silence,
absent themselves from the concerts,
awards ceremonies, listening chairs
of their other children.

I clear the spit valve, take a few breaths, start to play
the Christmas medley I'd been practicing for jazz band.
Get to the riff on "The Little Drummer Boy,"
who bangs, beats on his drum; don't let the irony
distract me from tonguing the tune correctly.

104

The drive Saturday morning is without incident.
Well medicated, Steven sits obligingly,
forehead tilted against the window,
focusing on the headrest of Dad's chair.

Dad makes no wrong turns.
By ten o'clock, Mom is urging Steven from the car and
up the well-swept brick steps that lead to the front door.

Everyone at Holland House is so *nice.*
Insanely compassionate,
morbidly understanding,
as we sit in their community room
with its soothing, gray-green walls,
chairs upholstered in inoffensive, symmetrical
blue-and-green squares.
No sharp edges anywhere.
Everything simple, subdued, ever-so-faintly piney.
It smells of anti-antiseptic,
as if whoever chose the stuff with which
they washed the tabletops, mopped the floors,

knew to avoid the aromas of ammonia, bleach.
Everything about this place is so mild, generic,
unremarkable;
so *nice*.

105

"Wasn't that fun, Steven?"
Mom chitters on the way home.
She makes no mention of the slap he gave the caretaker
who tried to put a crayon in his hand,
or the way I've chosen to ride home
in the third row of Dad's SUV
to avoid the edges of Steven's hand-twisting,
head-snapping attempts
at processing our unusual morning.

"Very nice people." Dad glances into the rearview
mirror. "Capable staff."

"And so clean. It smelled so fresh, didn't it, Daisy?"

I rub my unembellished eyes.
My late-night practice session made me too tired
to line them with kohl this morning.
The dark glaze on my nails has worn off at the edges.

My nails do not like the feel of polish.

It's as though they are being suffocated
under a layer of shellac.
Fingertips that cannot breathe surely can't play, I think.
And jazz band or no, I keep playing.
Ever since I picked up a horn
in the "mixed abilities" music class
to which Mom took Steven and me
when I was in third grade,
the trumpet has been part of me:
a layer, unlike polish, that I cannot chip away.

"It smelled piney," I say.

106

It's not quite two when I escape from home.
On the way to the Arts Center, I stop by Bouchard's
for a colossal cup of steaming Bear Mountain Blend,
sniff deep the smoky aroma that chases the smell
of sanitized evergreen from my nose.

"Cal tells me you haven't been in jazz band,"
Aggie greets me bluntly.

"Not Cal's business." I press my lips together.

"It's mine, though. I don't want to waste my time
teaching music
to somebody who won't share."

Dark brown roots divide Aggie's scalp from the shock of
white-yellow hair.
She is wearing a prim blue shirt and khaki slacks.

"What's with the outfit?"

She tugs at her L.L.Bean sleeves.
"I'm having dinner with my folks after this,
so I'm toning down the ink with some preppy."

I smile at my trumpet case,
consider designing a new bumper sticker—
"Tone Down That Ink with Some Preppy"—
on Mom's new color printer, something twisted,
contradictory in pink and green and black and purple.

"Everybody's telling me to get back to jazz band," I sigh.
But I don't make any promises,
just pick up my horn and play through tones and scales,
start in on the Ellington piece.
Let in the good feeling of someone hearing me play,
pretend I am sitting beside Miles Davis, John Coltrane,
sharing like Aggie said.

Even after banishing the pine smell with strong coffee,
it's hard to play away the vision of tepid colors,
studied smiles,
long corridors of beige linoleum tile.

My teacher listens awhile to my pallid playing,
her eyes thoughtful.
Then she unbuttons her blue oxford, shrugs it off

to reveal a much-more-Aggie tie-dyed T-shirt underneath,
and picks up her darling piccolo trumpet from its stand.
"Maybe what you need to do right now is keep sharing,
keep reaching
for that sound, even if so much around you seems wrong;
even if you feel lost and judged and sure of nothing."

She puts the trumpet to her lips
and launches into Louis Armstrong's "Wild Man Blues,"
one of our favorite tunes to improv together.
We play it clean, then jazz it up,
twist the melody, take turns showing off.
I don't even ask myself if Aggie will cover herself up again
before she sees her folks,
just let the rest of our hour roll by, faster than light yet
suspended in time
like the best improvs should be.

107

Packing up my trumpet case, I feel looser, lighter
than when I came into Aggie's practice room.

Until I see him sitting in the hall,
two sax cases on the floor by his chair.

"Nice to see you, Daisy." Cal stands up.
"Been a while since you've been at jazz band.
Is everything okay?"

"You had no right to talk to Aggie about that!
It's none of your business whether I come to jazz."

Cal toes the big bari sax case with his brown-laced shoe.
His forehead creases,
fair skin reddening just like Justine's does
when she isn't certain what mistake she's made.
"I didn't mean to upset you. Honest."

"I don't need anyone else trying
to keep me on a schedule, Cal O'Casey.

So you just go be a good boy and don't be late
for *your* lesson."

I sound like I am channeling
Ashleigh Anderson's condescending twang.
I feel bad, but I cannot stop.
Instead, I keep going, hip thrust out mean-girl style,
clutch my trumpet case in one hand,
and give him a dismissive little wave with the other.

Cal does not reply.
Just picks up his instruments,
crosses to the practice room threshold,
knocks on the door.

"Mornin' to ya, Miss Aggie. Ready to play?"
lilts back to my ears
as I turn, walk down the hall, out the door, to my car.

108

Dave gets to our house at ten past seven.
My parents hover in the doorway:
two greyhounds, ears cocked back,
listening for dangerous sounds from Steven,
whom they've planted in the family room,
watching a cartoon about cars.

"You remember Dave," I say.

He runs his hand through his hair.
"Hi, Mr. and Mrs. Meehan."

"Well, time to go."
My sneakered feet feel for the invisible line,
wonder if it will stop me
from dragging Dave down the walkway to his car.

"Sheesh, Daisy, you could've let me spend a minute
with your mom and dad.
Maybe say hi to Steven. I used to live right there."
He points to the house the Allen family lives in now,

with their two normal towheaded boys
and healthily chattering toddler daughter.

"Steven isn't like you remember him."

"What's he like?"

The trillion-dollar question.
If there were an answer,
the decision whether to nod and smile
when my parents admire
the clean, fresh smell of Holland House would be simple.

What "Steven" does Dave remember,
that he would dare to say hello?

I buckle my seat belt. "He's not too good. Let's go."

I reach for the radio, for once relieved
by the pounding beats of Dave's alt-rock station,
for the repetitive lyrics about wanting to get close,
not wanting to get burned,
that suddenly make total sense
and don't require conversation.

109

We're at the town park in ten minutes.
Dave pulls into a spot under the trees.

I don't wait
longer than it takes for him to turn off the Fiesta's
rumbly engine. I don't want
to join Belden and the crew I see in the distance
already clustered around a fire
they've built in one of the community barbecues.

"I brought marshmallows for the s'mores."
He gestures to a grocery bag in the back seat.

"It looks cold out there," I say.
Instead of opening my door,
I clamber over the gear shift onto his lap.
"And I've had such a long day."

He gives me a funny grin, puts a hand on my cheek.
"You always surprise me, Daisy."

"What? Not Daisy-brains right now?"
I press my face into the heat of his palm.

In answer, he draws me to him.

Every kiss sends a tingling thrill deeper
into my chest, my stomach, down.

I want "Adult Content."
I want "Some Nudity."
I don't want to be the town's-pride-trumpeter,
Accepted two years running to Honor Band of America
(I didn't apply this year
since Mom is afraid to be home alone).
I want to be neither reliable nor extraordinary;
neither sound nor silence,
but just a girl kissing a tousle-haired bad boy.
I want to be *now.*

I let my lips open, feel Dave's tongue connect with mine.
Condensation clouds over the car windows.
Straddling his lap, I slide my hands to the buttons of his shirt.

He puts his hands over mine, finishes unbuttoning,
shrugs it off.

I tug my sweater over my head,
struggle out of the second sleeve.
The clack of my watch against the driver's side window
makes me giggle.

Dave gives a growling laugh.
His lips move from my mouth down the side of my neck
to my shoulder.
His warm hands slide up to my breasts,
so I have to arch my back to keep kissing him.

I think I would do anything to forget today,
to make time stop now, this night.
But maybe it's regret for wearing practical,
laceless underwear or the dropping temperature outside
that makes this more difficult than our first time at the lake.

I press against Dave,
feeling for that stilling magic in the heat of his skin.
Try to close my mind to the picture
of Justine doing this with Ned;
to the image of my parents sitting angrily on the couch,
waiting for my return;
to the worry that someone from the bonfire by the lake
can see us through the steaming car windows.

As Dave reaches behind to undo my bra,
there's a thump on the roof of the car.

"Hey, Miller."
It's jack-in-the-box Josh Belden,
popping over to cool our heat once again.
"You gonna pony up some marshmallows?"

"Get away!" I shriek, flailing for my sweater.

Dave wraps calming arms around me.
"Give us a couple minutes, okay?"

"Shit, sorry man."
Belden retreats to the waterside.

I crumple onto the front seat floor,
try to scramble back into my clothes,
as desperate to get away from this humiliation
as I am determined not to go home.

Dave lines up the buttons of his shirt.
"You okay down there?"

"I'm, uh, I'm fine."

"Do you want to get out of here?" he asks.

"I don't know."
I retie the right, black-heart-and-red-diamond-
embellished Ked, which has somehow come unlaced.

"Belden didn't see anything," he assures me.
"And he wouldn't say anything anyway."

"Do you remember in second grade,
that time my tights got stuck . . . ?"

Even in the dim light cast by the faraway fire,
I can see the flash of Dave's carelessly hot grin.
"Wouldn't admit it if I did."

Past the bonfire crowd,
the full moon is suspended marshmallow-white
over the blue-black water.

110

Sweater straightened,
I slide back up onto the passenger seat,
turn on the radio.
A thumping rap recounts things that are hot, irresistible.
I wish there wasn't a party at the pits,
or that Dave hadn't brought me here—
that we were alone together
somewhere.

He turns down the volume, lets out a long breath.
"This was not what I expected from tonight."
He tries to take my hand.

A wave of anger makes me cross my arms over my chest.
"What were you expecting?
If you want more than a make-out buddy,
you have to ask a girl on a real date,
with a restaurant reservation and a menu.
Not marshmallows and Belden's brew."

"I didn't mean . . . Shit, Daisy,

I was hoping we could be . . ."

"Be what?" My face feels like fire.
"Playground pals again? We're seventeen years old.
You've barely talked to me since grade school.
Then these past few weeks . . . I don't understand.
You're a badass slacker and I'm a band geek
with a totally messed-up family."

"Don't play the messed-up family card with me!"
I am not used to the steely glint in his eyes.
"When we were still playing on the swings, everyone
in this town knew my mom was screwing around.
Except me."

"I didn't," I lie,
just like Justine after my flubbed solo with the orchestra,
even as I remember Mom and Dad
discussing the messy Miller marriage
at our own kitchen table,
back when Steven was small enough to manage
and my parents believed their love for each other
was built of steel, not sand.

"I'm gonna bring the marshmallows down to Belden."
Dave's voice is cold with disbelief.

He gets out of the car, slams the door a little too hard.

Is it wrong to tweak the pitch of memories
so the bad ones don't play in our hearts in minor keys?

How does Jasper choose
which of its townspeople's many unsecret secrets
to keep?

Why do I cling so hard to the echo of Ned
laughing at my upturned skirt
but let myself forget that feeling, after hours spent
pushing cars alongside Steven,
of him pelting the little metal toys at my head,
my back—
how I would run to Mom, bury my face in her shoulder,
and both she and I would cry?

What was Dave hoping we could be?

The question leads me down to the lake.
"Sorry I got so angry," I whisper to Dave.
"Things are bad at home."

He hands me a marshmallow speared onto a sharp twig,
gently kisses the top of my head. "Don't get burned."

I lean against his shoulder,
still afraid to ask what he wants,
what he wanted that very first day I caught him waiting
outside the band room at school,
because I'm not sure what answer I'd want him to give me.
What truth.
What lie.

We let words fall away,
just laugh when every other marshmallow
erupts into flames,
pull our sleeves over our hands so the cold beer bottles
don't freeze our fingers.
Until I finally feel ready for Dave to take me home.

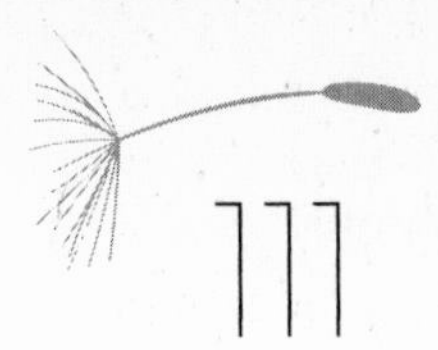

111

The house is quiet when I get home.
Mom has fallen asleep on the living room couch,
a sweaty, muscle-bound guy on the television
promising her rock-hard abs
in twenty minutes a day.

I don't wake her. Just hit the TV "off" button,
switch off the lights,
tiptoe up the stairs.

Gentle snores slide under the door of Steven's bedroom.

Before the divorce,
before the room was repainted in girl-power pink,
Justine and I used to sneak into her dad's office
where, hidden in a bottom drawer,
he kept his *Playboy* magazines
and one inexplicable *Playgirl*,
which we explored to tatters.

I try to imagine Dave

beneath his flannel boxers, low-slung jeans,
looking like one of those baby-oiled photographs;
think of Steven,
how often, now,
his hands stray into his pants.
It drives my mother crazy,
uncertain whether to reprimand or ignore,
or cry.

Is Steven any different from me?
What does his mind do when his fingers travel there?
Does he imagine, with the sensation,
a face,
a loyalty?
Does he fear a betrayal?
A lust unrequited by love?

112

I should be more elated by Dave's Sunday morning text:
"Missing you till Monday."

Steven's waffle unburnt,
routines in place, Dad spends the morning
repairing the cracked kitchen drywall.
He stays with Mom after lunch,
so I can go down to the basement
and start trumpet practice before the sun sets.

It feels like a day in the normal house
I sometimes dream about.

113

"We visited one of those autism homes
for Steven this weekend,"
I admit to Justine as we drive to school Monday morning.

"What was it like?"

"I don't know. Clean. Calm. It seemed okay."
The subject pinches like a new pair of shoes,
but each time I take a step, give up a few words,
the leather of my pain stretches,
makes a little more room for me to breathe.

"Clean is good. More than can be said for my bedroom,"
Justine says.

I smile. "Yep, you're a slob."

"Ned can't stand the clutter.
I swear, he tries to fold my clothes
every time he comes through the door."

"*Every* time?"

She blushes.

We pull up to a parking spot
right by the front entrance of Evergreen High.
Lunch is teriyaki beef and sautéed carrots—not bad.
After, Dave invites me to hang out behind the school
and I go,
closing my mind to the "A-absent" and "T-tardy"
symbols accumulating on my attendance record,
to A-PUSH's imaginary Jeremy
and my neglected real-life tutee, Cal.

We don't talk about Saturday night;
just watch the high clouds floating over the playground,
agree on our hopes for Thanksgiving snow,
kiss enough to make me late for concert band class.

114

"Daisy, I have e-mailed both your parents and yourself.
No one has replied about your absences from zero period."

Even though the class has started,
Mr. Orson comes out to talk to me in the hall.
His eyes, full of gentle concern,
take in my heavy-shaded lids,
my unembellished black sneakers.

"I haven't stopped practicing, Mr. O," I assure him.

"This isn't like you. Mrs. Pendleton told
me your parents are making some"—
he hesitates—"changes at home."

I stumble backward,
more stunned than if he'd slapped me.
My Monday charade of gorgeous normalcy is shattered.

"Changes,"
I whisper inside my head.

Seven harsh letters ricochet round my skull.
I try to quiet my heaving chest,
wait for some answer, any words at all,
to will their way to my lips.
"Then you know why."

"I wish I could let you take more time.
But I can't falsify the attendance record,
and if you have too many unexcused absences,
you'll be automatically failed."
He puts a hand on my shoulder.
"The jazz band needs you.
I think you need them, too."

He smiles, but I can't smile back.
Behind him
I see every concert band member's eyes
boring curiously through the interior window,
watching us.

I bend down, pretending to fix my sneaker lace, whisper
the knife-word that's never been wielded at me before:
"Failed."
It feels strangely satisfying—different,
like my dramatic eyes. Kind of easy, too—
not so much an action

as a nonaction, a silence, a not-being-there.

"You know," Mr. Orson continues,
"I wrote some glowing recommendations for you this fall.
I never imagined you were the kind of person
who would give up music
just because other parts of your life got difficult.
I pegged you as one who would, despite anything,
hold on."

"I thought so, too," I whisper,
eyes focused self-protectively inward.
I straighten my back, lift my chin,
try to channel Justine
as I follow him into the band room.

115

"Want to come with us for coffee at Bouchard's?"
Ned asks after school,
too quickly for Justine to shush him,
his mouth moving before he realized
the invitation he's extended is to the girl
who is kissing Andy Bouchard's trophy wife's son.

"Or we could go for ice cream."
Justine tries to pull my fingers from my car door handle.
"Unless you're waiting for Dave."

"I should probably get home."
I toss my backpack into the passenger seat.
An inexplicable surge of worry passes through me.

"Call me later. We'll talk."
Justine's expression assures me
she hasn't spoken of Steven to Ned,
which makes me smile with gratitude
even as I press my foot hard on the gas pedal,
slide through the four-way stop sign without braking.

There's a police car outside our house, lights flashing.
And an ambulance.

Mrs. Allen from up the street stands in our front yard,
her toddler daughter balanced on her hip.
"I heard your mother scream. I called 911.
She's in there now."
She points.

Mom is on a stretcher in the back.
A uniformed EMT kneels beside her.

"I told your dad I'd watch for your car,
let you know what happened."

"Wait for me," I yell to the medic.
"I'll ride to the hospital with her."
I dash through the open front door.
The hall is littered with broken glass,
strewn with sprays of dried flowers.
Through the kitchen entryway I glimpse Steven
flailing against the locking embrace of Dad's angry arms
as I run back out to the bright-red van.

116

Dad kisses Mom gingerly
when we come through the front door five hours later.
He has managed to get Steven to take a pill
that will make him sleep.
"You okay?"

"I'm . . . fine."
The bruise over Mom's left eye is getting darker.

"Guess you don't need me anymore," I say,
heading for the stairs.
I want to practice, but I feel too tired.

"Thanks for coming with me, Daisy," Mom says.

Her left forearm is in a cast.
I wonder how she'll do yoga.

"No problem," I reply.

They are right.

They are right.
They are right.

We cannot live like this.
We have to let Steven go.
They are right, but I don't want it to be true.

Where is the normal,
the hope I felt when I woke up this morning?

I text Dave: "Can you come get me?"

"Where do you want to go?" he texts back.

"Anywhere but here."

"Fifteen minutes."

117

I wonder if Steven realizes the die he has cast,
whether tomorrow at the breakfast table
I will see in his expression remorse, regret.
And if I do, will it be there or just a lie I want to believe?

I remember when Dad used to tuck me into bed at night.
He'd tell me a list of things he loved about me:
my smile, my laugh,
the music I made, the silly jokes I told,
the way I loved to read stories about animals,
baby bunnies, tiny turtles.
I'd wrap my arms around him, say, "I love you, Daddy,"
never asking what was on the list he made for my brother,
who didn't smile, didn't joke, didn't say "I love you."

I, too, have started something I cannot stop
by calling Dave, not Justine.
Instead of confiding in my best friend
that the unthinkable has happened again,
I will have to tell Dave
what happened to Mom, what Steven has done.
What lie could I offer instead?

Flakes of snow are falling when the Fiesta pulls up—
the pretty kind that won't stick
to the not-quite-frozen ground,
just linger for seconds on your hair, your tongue,
melt away without consequence.

"You okay, Daisy?"

"No."

"Where do you want to go?"

I wish the library were open.
Dave and I could sit hip to hip in the egg chair
in the middle of the fiction section
and just be without a yesterday, without a tomorrow.
"I guess down to the lake."

"You told me that's not a real date."

"This isn't a date," I tell him.
"I just need to get away from the house."

"I get that."
He drives to the end of my street and turns onto Main.

118

"Looks like we might have a White Thanksgiving
after all," Dave says.
He has driven us past the parking lot,
down to the boat launch at the lake's edge,
vacant on this cold November Monday.

"It's not going to stick."

"Don't be so hopeless," he says,
sliding his fingers between mine.

We sit there, holding hands,
watching innocent snowflakes
dissolve into the dark blue water.

"A little jazz?" he points to the radio.

"The quiet is nice."
I wonder if we can sit this way forever,
or at least until the car runs out of gas.
Cozy against the worn leather upholstery,

lulled by the friendly rumble of the old engine,
I hold the moment like a fragile glass,
like how my father kissed my mother.

"The other night," Dave says at last,
"you asked me what I was expecting from you."

"I thought maybe you didn't know."

He gives his hair a familiar nervous rumple.
"I don't want
to be the odd one out at my dad's anymore;
I want a place like the sandbox we used to play in,
where you and I were safe,
felt like nothing would ever change."

He hasn't asked what he was rescuing me from—
why I needed to get away.

"I'm a person, not a place. And we've already changed.
You ditched me when you moved across town.
I made other friends, got good at music, grew boobs!"
My voice is rising to a shout,
the kind that would send Steven into spirals of fury.

Steven . . .

Steven . . .

"Steven broke my mother's arm!"
Those words come out loudest of all.
Dave wraps his arms around me,
nestles my head beneath his chin.
Trickling teardrops grow to a storm of drenching sobs
until I can no longer see the frosty lake before me
and Dave Miller's chest is soaked in my snotty anguish.

119

Comfort turns to kissing,
hard and desperate,
although I don't repeat the mistake of climbing into his lap.

I tell myself it's okay that I feel more anger than romance.
If HBO is right, I am allowed my lust,
like so many fickle fantasy vixens and powerful mafia men.
I am discovering a new talent
for disappearing into touch, taste,
not unlike losing myself in sound.

Dave wraps his arm around my ribs,
like he did that first time we kissed
in the parking lot of Evergreen High.

This time, I am not frightened
by the tightness of the embrace.
I know it is different from when I am touched by Steven.
Dave isn't trying to drive some wordless message
into my bones.

He isn't hurting me.

He is holding on.

120

Dave can't keep hold of my hand for the drive home.
He grips the wheel against roads that have turned slick.
The grass on the yards we pass is laced in white.
The snow is beginning to stick.

"Want me to walk you in?" he asks
as I open the passenger-side door.

I put one Ked gingerly on the driveway to test for ice.
"No. I'm okay."

"Is it . . . safe?"

"Safe enough. We've been living this way
for a long time."
Another honest note blows into the air.
"I'll see you tomorrow."

I watch the Fiesta ease back down the driveway,
steel myself for what's behind my front door.

121

Mom is tucked beneath a blanket on the couch,
her busted arm elevated on pillows.
After he hurts her, she's afraid to sleep upstairs,
close to Steven.

Dad looks up from his recliner.
He makes no comment about my being out past ten
on a school night;
just says grimly,
"It's all set. There's an open respite bed at Holland House.
They can take Steven on Wednesday.
I'm taking a couple of days off.
Not a big deal since it's Thanksgiving on Thursday.
It's a quiet week at the office.
I'll handle things here."

I think back to a few mornings ago,
Steven shrinking from my touch, ignoring my question
of whether he understands.
I wonder what pain he must have felt,
to make him lash out at Mom.

But that does not make his actions any less dangerous.
And one word describes the rush of feeling
that courses through my arms and legs,
fingers and toes,
heart and brain.
It is *relief.*

122

In the morning, it is Dad bustling at the sink
while Mom sits at the island
holding a cup of tea in her uncast hand.

Like the past times when Steven's violence exploded
out of control,
this next morning feels extraordinarily . . . ordinary.
He is tired from the meds,
his hands twist more slowly than usual,
evenly cut waffle bites sit untouched
on the plate before him.

It is hard to bear the glimmer of hope in Mom's eyes
as she watches Steven be still,
as if she has already begun the process of pretending
yesterday never was.
Maybe that's the most painful thing of all.

"Mind if I stay over at Justine's tonight?" I ask.

Dad's "Are you afraid?"

and Mom's "Don't you want to spend time with Steven?"
tumble over each other, both easily answered
with a single syllable: "No."

Stomach growling, sleepover gear in hand, I skip cereal
and go straight out the front door to the Subaru.
The "eventually" of Steven's departure
is now twenty-four hours away.

The gas indicator is down to two bars,
but I still run the engine in the Evergreen High
parking lot, blast the heat until I can't bear it
any more than I can bear waiting at home with my parents
for tomorrow to arrive.

Ten minutes before the bell, I turn off the ignition,
creep through the school halls
like the spy I sometimes pretend to be.
I miss the Christmas tunes, the joy,
the sound of the program getting better as we get closer
and closer to concert dates,
the full, round tones of the Evergreen High Jazz Band,
complete with baritone sax.

Dave comes up behind me.
"Why aren't you in there playing?"

"I just haven't felt like it."

"If I were as good at something
as you are at trumpet,
I don't think that excuse would be enough."

"You sound like Ned Hoffman. Parental," I sneer.

"Suit yourself." He shrugs.
"With all the shit going on at your house,
I'd think you'd love to just go make some music."

I've gone a long time trying to love
a brother whose only way of touching me is pain.
A long time escaping into music.
Practice, lessons, rehearsals that protect me
from the hurting parts of life.
I've been winning awards, applause,
acclaim for my trumpet skills since I was in grade school.

But *love*?
The word catches in my throat.
Do I love anything?
Have I forgotten how?

123

"Daisy!" Justine calls.
She tugs Ned along by the hand,
gives Dave and me an appraising glance.
"I'm so psyched you're sleeping over tonight!"

Her voice is party-light, her words innocent,
but I see the sharp compassion in her eyes,
searching for what I need, what hurts.

"What'll it be, Scrabble tournament
or reality TV marathon?" she asks.

"I've had my fill of reality," I say
in what I hope is both witty
and a nothing-ever-really-troubles-me-or-if-it-does-
I'm-not-telling-boys tone.
"Let's make up words."

124

I do not go home
to say good-bye to Steven on Wednesday morning.
There was a plan,
a story to tell Steven
about the fun of going back to that nice place,
to piney-smelling, soft-edged Holland House,
and how we would come "soon" to see him.
I am afraid he'll read the confusion in my face.
I know none of us will try to hug him good-bye.
I can imagine the ordeal of tying his shoes,
getting him into Dad's car.
I do not need to bear witness.
I do not go to jazz band either.

Justine and I sit at her kitchen table
eating bowls of banned-at-my-house Cap'n Crunch
while Shirley chatters about feeling bad
that Mom plans to go to all the trouble
of cooking Thanksgiving dinner tomorrow,
what with her broken arm and . . . everything.

To me, it is a perfect irony.
Thanksgiving is loaded with falsehoods,
from the candy-apple way they teach kindergartners
that the pilgrims met the Native Americans
to the stage-play that is barely speaking families
gathering to pretend
they are thankful for the gift of their genetic connections,
even if they hate the hell out of each other.

At school, Dave tells me
he has to spend Thanksgiving weekend
at Andy Bouchard's farm outside of town
with his mom.
He doesn't say he hates her. I don't think he does.
But there's no contesting she was the catalyst
for the destruction of the Miller family—
the old one,
before his father's new wife,
the twin baby girls Dave never wants to care for.
I imagine his dad, nearing fifty,
staring at the two diapered toddlers
like my own father watches Steven, his eternal child,
the thief of his retirement fund,
his chances at ever claiming a reward
for the years of hard work;
dashed by a mind that cannot love back,

that will never grow to own similar hopes,
or fulfill his father's.

What is a family anyway?
Do we all have to live in one house?
I think of Justine and her mom,
who have bravely come to our house for Thanksgiving
every year since Shirley's divorce,
the same year my grandparents begged off joining us
for the holiday,
claiming they caused Steven too much distress,
even if the only pain I ever saw was in their eyes
when they looked at me and Dad and Mom.

So, are Justine and Shirley my family?
The people who gather round our table,
who actually dare to love us despite everything?

125

The house is empty when I get home after school.

I pour myself a bowl of cereal
and head to the family room.

HBO is offering a steamy blend
of high crime and hookers
that would normally be my ideal type of evening fare,
though with accents is preferable.

But tonight, I flip to a cartoon,
study the bright colors, stylized animation,
realize I can turn the volume up if I want to.
But I don't.

It has happened and the only stand I took
was not to stop them
but to stop the music in myself.

I hate them for not noticing,
until I hear the front door open,

the shuddering sobs of my mother,
the falsely reassuring, “It’s going to be okay, Alice.
We’re going to be okay,” from my father.

I run to the basement like a programmed robot,
and it’s not until my second time through “Hallelujah”
that I realize I could have played the song upstairs.

The song about the imperfection of love,
the way it can hurt you, break you, terrify you;
the way it can fall apart; and yet,
the title is a hymn, a word of praise.

I wonder if my mother has retreated to the shower,
if my father is in the guest room bed,
or if, maybe, he’ll stay in the master tonight.

I wonder . . .

Did we try hard enough?
Did I?

126

PTSD is in the news a lot these days:
post-traumatic stress disorder,
a diagnosis often given
to soldiers returning home from Iraq, Afghanistan, war.
Probably should've been given to Civil War veterans, too.
Now I understand
how it feels to be thrust out of your familiar world
of danger and chaos
into sudden quiet.
Into a home absent of dangers,
sheltered beneath a blanket of falling snow.

"Want me to move the music stand up to your bedroom?"
Dad asks on Thursday night,
after the turkey leftovers are stashed in the fridge
without a bowl of mac and cheese beside them,
after the unbroken dishes are washed
and Justine and Shirley head out to the Hoffmans' house
for pumpkin pie.

"No thanks."

Zombielike, I get my backpack from the hall closet,
stack my A-PUSH textbook and binder
neatly on the kitchen table. Pretend to be reading
instead of trying to imagine the sound of a trumpet
filling up this house.
What would I play?
Would Mom peel carrots,
scrub pans to the Hummel concerto?
Would Dad stop his early morning runs and, instead,
read the paper, drink his coffee
as I wind around improvisations to suit my mood
and no one else's?

What would the sounds of liberty be?

I click open a pen and scribble down some notes
for Cal's and my project
about the stunned, uncertain way a slave might feel,
suddenly free,
realizing the story I am trying to tell isn't about Steven.
It's about me.

127

"I missed the Black Friday sales," Mom says at breakfast.
"But I'm going to see what's left on the shelves today."

"Maybe I'll go to the gym. Or just watch some TV,"
Dad says from behind his paper.

We are all hiding
from the ugliness of our relief,
from the countless uncircumscribed hours
that now lay before us.
Dad sits still long enough for me to notice
the tufts of gray at his temples.
Mom isn't running from the table to the sink,
away from danger, from Steven.
I think of movies I have seen about tsunamis, hurricanes,
where, after the storm has passed,
there's this brilliant blue sky, clear horizon,
scored by the music of memory, of grief,
of what was lost,
and it all seems to happen so fast.

I think I have aged ten years since Wednesday.
Without benefit of HBO makeup,
I've gone from third parent to old woman,
wondering at the absurdity of my ink-addled shoes,
exhausted by the notion of burying my thoughts
in sweaty scenes of tousled hair and breathless kisses.
Very, very tired.

"What's your plan, Daisy?"
Mom maintains her falsely bright, steady tone
as if Steven were still here,
in need of hearing the day's narrative repeated.

"I'm going to do some homework, then practice.
Maybe meet up with Justine later."

Dad looks up from his paper and smiles his approval.

"I don't know if we can afford it,
but I applied to the Overton summer music program
in Philadelphia."
It feels like a confession.

"I thought I wrote a check for a Boston camp,"
Mom says, confused.

"I applied to lots of programs. I wanted to . . ."
There must be a word to capture all the reasons—
the musical inspirations, the dreams of escape,
from routines, from fighting parents, from fear—
but I can't find it.
And I realize that, whatever that word might be,
my parents have surely felt it, known it, too.
So I finish simply.
". . . to go."

"What programs?"
Dad actually sets his paper down on the table.

"Well, Overton, of course.
Then there's one in upstate New York, and . . ."

"How much do they cost?" he asks.

"They're all, well, thousands, and I know
you've got a lot of expenses now.
If I get in, I can try for scholarships."

"I'm sure you'll get in."
I see Mom smile over my head at Dad,
her eyes full of pride.

"We'll do the best we can, Daisy," Dad says.
"Let's see how things go with Steven."

Can you be miserable and relieved
to hear someone say your brother's name,
to keep him somehow in the house
even though you've sent him away?

128

Dad leaves for the gym,
Mom heads to the sales.

The emptiness in the house is so loud, I can't stay.
I grab my keys and jump into the Subaru.
The tank is nearly empty.
I pull into a gas station off the highway,
slide my credit card in the slot, type in my zip code, remove the gas cap.
Pumping gas usually makes me feel confident, capable.
Now, as I hear the gentle swish of fluid through the nozzle,
turn my face from the breeze carrying gasoline-scented air,
I am stranded in the eternal measure
that followed the wrong note I played
at the state orchestra concert.

The absence of Steven is a conductor's dropped baton,
a Christmas score burned by the high school bleachers.
Changes too fast to survive.

Car replenished, I drive straight to Justine's.

I don't need permission from Mom or Dad,
don't need to feel guilt—
only now I do.

129

"How are you doing, honey?"

Shirley wraps me in a hug before I can unzip my fleece.

"Okay," I say.

Justine meets us in the doorway. "Honestly, Mom.
Do you think she needs the third degree right now?"

I do adore Justine's flashing defenses.

"Wanna go up to your room?" I ask.

"Yeah." She gives her mother
one final reprimanding look
and we head upstairs.

The pink bedspread is buried, as usual, under a sea
of clothes and shoes.
I shove aside a pair of shiny pumps and sit on the edge.

"It's really quiet at home," I say.

She sits down beside me,
on a cute lavender top,
not even bothering to push it out of the way.
After a long time, she stands up.
"Well, let's not make it quiet here.
Maybe you should, you know,
do a little more socializing,
try to enjoy some of the traditions of junior year."

"Like the Black-and-White Dance?" I tease weakly.

"Well, yeah. Why don't you ask someone?
Maybe Dave?" She studies my face, retreats a little.
"Though you guys have a weird history."

"What history?" Ned knocks on Justine's door
and comes in at the same time.

"Ned! You scared me. We're thinking
of someone Daisy could ask to the dance."

"No, we weren't."
I'm squirming now, a little angry,
definitely not ready for this,
for Ned brainstorming potential dates for me.

"How about Cal O'Casey?" Ned suggests.
"You and he are both music people."
His hands are on Justine's shoulders, rubbing her back.

I leap off the bed.
"You have no right to butt into my social life, Ned;
to try to manipulate me
like you manipulate the ladies of the PTA.
Do you even remember that time in second grade
when you laughed at me
but didn't tell me my dress was in my tights;
just let me walk all the way back to my desk?"

"Daisy!" Justine pulls away from Ned, glaring at me.

"You remember, Justine.
You slept over at my house that night
and listened to me cry about it."

"That was second grade!" she actually screams.
"People change!
Look at Dave."

Ned, frozen amidst the clothes and pink and screaming,
looks like he's grown suddenly thinner,

more shadowlike than before.
"I remember." His whisper fights its way
through the chaos.

"Ned?" Justine turns to him.

"I was . . . embarrassed.
I didn't know how to talk to girls.
I'm . . . sorry."
He lifts his hand as if to reach out to me,
drops it back to his side, his head lowered.

That word again,
sorry.
That word I want to say to my brother,
even if he doesn't understand.
That word I believe Ned Hoffman really means right now.
And I realize that we are the same,
that sometimes we don't have the strength
to rescue other people;
sometimes we have to learn things for ourselves, first.

Someday, down the road, I will be the adult,
will make the decisions for Steven.
Even if I don't have much faith
that my brother will change,

even if Steven isn't able to forgive me for my choices, the way I decide, now, to forgive Ned.

130

Time feels like it needs to be counted
in days-since-Steven-was-sent-away.
And none of them feels any better than the last.
Ignoring Mr. Orson's lecture
about coming back to jazz band,
on Monday I play all day
in my basement practice room,
a prisoner of myself,
ignoring texts from Justine, from Dave.
Mom doesn't make me go to school.

Tuesday, I wince as the sun attacks my eyes.
Mom stands by my bedroom window,
straightening the freshly drawn shade.

"Enough," she says. "We have to find a way to go on."

She has put a cereal bowl, a spoon, a glass of orange juice
at my usual spot on the kitchen island.

Dad comes down the stairs, smiles at us,

says three amazing words:
"Good morning, Alice."

"Good morning, Ted." Mom smiles back,
kind of hopeful.
"You'd better hurry, Daisy. You'll be late for jazz band."

I park the Subaru near the school
but leave my horn in the car.
Walk empty-handed down the halls, still quiet
except for zero-period students:
the Young Entrepreneurs group, choir, jazz band.

Cal is leaning against his locker.

"What's the holdup, O'Casey?
You're gonna be late for jazz."

He shrugs. "Dunno if it matters. I'm gonna just listen
when you run the Ellington piece, anyway,
since I won't be here for Battle of the Bands."

"Why not?"

He looks down,
Cal-for-short's-first-day-at-Evergreen style.

"Mrs. Ackerman is pregnant, home on bed rest,
and they can't handle a student boarder
after the holidays.
My folks were so set against me comin' here already;
now I don't have a place and . . ."
Cal's voice catches in his throat. He turns away.
"I shouldn't stay.
Dad's gettin' old and Jeremy, my brother, is only seven.
Without me to take over,
Dad'll probably have to sell the pub.
So it isn't like he can pay for me to rent someplace
even if I dared ask him to stay.
Hell, I came to America with only one pair of shoes!"

I know everything about this feeling:
trapped by family, a sea of obligations.
"Oh, Cal."

"Daisy, is that what I have to do?
Go home and live my whole life in that place
so Dad doesn't have to take the name O'Casey's off
from over the door?"

"Couldn't you go to music school someplace in Ireland?
I'm sure if—"

"Y' don't understand.
The minute I walk back into that pub,
he'll slap an apron on me
and I'll be washin' pint glasses in the kitchen again,
my dreams pissin' down the drain with the rinse water."

"This isn't the end yet, Cal. Not today."
I don't know how to help him, but I know how it feels
to have your hopelessness come from home.
A twinge of Justine's angry fire rises in my stomach
along with a little bit of hope
that a way can be found for Cal.
"Today, we play 'Almost Cried'
by the great Duke Ellington, but we . . .
we do not cry."

That's when I go back to my car,
take out my trumpet case,
return, Cal in tow, just a little bit late
to jazz band.

131

It's the push to perfect the Christmas carols
for the holiday concert.

I hesitate at the door
as the final round of "Good King Wenceslas" ends
on a long, slow note.

"Nice to see you, Daisy." Mr. Orson waves his hand.
I put my music on the stand, unpack my trumpet,
grin at the back of Dave's head,
brown hair mushed against the outside
of the music room window.

It's like I've never left
the only place that feels like it hasn't changed.

132

Lunch is chicken burger and kernel corn,
Ned and Justine making out inches from my tray,
Cal, who has joined us,
looking studiously in any other direction.

Cal's troubles—
Mrs. Ackerman and the threat of returning to Ireland—
are still his secrets,
though I think maybe if he asked Jasper,
the town might reach out to help.

It is hard to know when it's right to be silent
and when it's right to make noise.
I chew, muse,
watch prom-queen-purposeful Ashleigh Anderson
taping signs
announcing the upcoming Black-and-White Dance
along the cafeteria walls. As soon as she leaves
to plaster the rest of the halls,
Josh Belden starts pulling the flyers down
with equal enthusiasm.

"Hey, Daisy-brains, comin' out back?"

It's Dave, with his tray,
a tantalizing glimmer in his eye.

Beside me,
I half feel, half see Ned and Justine exchange a look.

I'm pushed and pulled,
wanting to bury myself in the timelessness
of Dave's eager kisses
but tired of not knowing
what's going on between us,
feeling a little uncertain, a little unsafe,
like I'm driving toward a bend in the road
with no idea of what lies beyond the curve.

In jazz, letting go of the melody,
finding your own way through a tune, feels beautiful,
free;
I want being with Dave to feel the same.

Instead I am jealous of Justine and Ned,
tempted to kiss Cal,
mostly because I'm pretty sure he would kiss me back.

What I want to feel is Dave
clear and for certain—
not like this.

"I really can't have any more tardies
on my attendance record."
I try to smile a please-see-through-this-tough-act-and-tell-me-what-we-are smile,
but that's a complicated expression
and Dave's toss of his overgrown bangs,
his straight-backed turn-on-heel,
makes me pretty sure I've failed.

133

The folks at Holland House told Mom
Steven wasn't settled in enough for a family visit yet,
but she and Dad head out early Wednesday morning
all the same.
"Even," Mom says, "if all I get to do
is glimpse the back of him through a window."

I guess everyone has his or her own way of coping.
Some go, some stay.

I managed one day at school,
but two in a row seems impossible.
I picture jazz band, homeroom, A-PUSH,
like Civil War daguerreotypes,
artifacts from an ancient life,
preceding a present I am unable to endure.

Still in my pajamas, I crawl downstairs to the family room,
watch, unseeing, as HBO offers
some happy movie about pioneering teachers.
At ten, the doorbell, already adjusted by Dad

to a Steven-less higher volume, startles me.

I wrap my pajama top tighter around me,
creep to the front door. Skip over formal niceties.

"Shouldn't you be at school, Cal?"

"Shouldn't you?"

I step aside to let Cal pass,
see him take in our polished hardwood,
white-painted moldings,
the tufted leather couch in the living room to the right.

"I didn't mean to be rude," Cal continues.
"I mean, I heard, o' course, about your brother."

"Who hasn't?" My arms unfurl,
my flannel pajamas flutter loose around my middle.
"Nothing is ever sacred in Jasper.
Sometimes I just hate this town."

"I dunno. It's nice when people care.
Everyone's so proud of your music.
Mrs. Ackerman even showed me a YouTube video
of you playing your trumpet on some PBS program

when you were ten years old."
He stops, as if re-watching it in his mind.

"Wow." I try to seem offhanded,
but I think I'm turning as pink as the Irish boy.
"I haven't heard a compliment in a while."

He gives a funny little nod, stiff and proper.

"Come in. I'm gonna get dressed.
You can wait here."

He sits at the kitchen island, watches
while I start some coffee.

Up in my room, I slip into jeans, a sweatshirt,
a pair of yellow Keds
emblazoned with powder-blue quarter notes.

The coffee is brewed when I get back downstairs.
I fill two mugs,
sit in the second wrought-iron barstool at the island.

"Maybe we could work on the Civil War project,"
I suggest.

"I dunno. It seems a waste to do homework since
I doubt I'll be goin' to Evergreen High much longer.
Even though the place feels like freedom to me
compared t' my life in Dublin."

"Any luck finding a new place to stay?" I ask.

He sips his coffee, shakes his head, expression grim.
"Took ages to get Da to let me come to America
on this exchange program.
Figured, once I got here, I'd find a way to stay . . ."

His watercolor blue eyes are wet with dreams
and sorrows
and maybe a little loneliness—
more emotion, expression,
than a face has borne in my family's kitchen
for a long, long time.

"*Slavery*'s a complicated word, isn't it?
You ran away from a kind of slavery.
It's been only a week since I—
Since my parents and I have been set free
from my brother."

"Worst thing about coming to America

is missin' my little brother, Jeremy.
But maybe you understand?"
His expression isn't nosy, just curious.
And for once, I don't feel angry.

"Explaining autism is like trying to put the way you
hold your lips, your cheeks,
the way you breathe to buzz into the trumpet, into words.
The only true understanding is inside,
once you've made the sound yourself.
I can't explain what living with Steven was like
any more than I will be able to understand
what happens in Steven's mind,
but I can tell you, even though it was frightening,
having him gone . . . well, it hurts."

"I wonder," Cal says. "If we could write about our slave,
the way he misses others from the plantation he fled.
How there was happiness there,
even if it came without freedom.
There was family."

134

We don't work on our project;
just sit in companionable silence, sipping coffee,
letting honesty settle around us,
like the snow that begins to fall outside.

"Look!" I point at the flakes outside the kitchen window.
"Let's go!"

He follows me out the back door.
Coatless and shivering, we watch fat flakes hit the ground.
This time, I think, it's going to stick.

This time, I think,
I can make it through two days of jazz band,
maybe three in a row.

I scoop my hand along the patio table, collecting
the thin layer of wet snow that has collected there;
pack it into a ball.
Toss it at Cal, who turns, takes it full on the mouth.

"Hey, no fair!"

"Were there rules?"
I tease, running toward the back fence.
He catches me round the waist, spins me,
rubbing a fistful of snow into my hair.

I am giggling when I see a long shadow
in the corner of our yard.

"Who's there?" I call out,
joy replaced by horror-movie panic.

I chase the shadow around to the front yard
in time to see a Ford Fiesta veer
backward out of my driveway,
too fast for the unplowed road.

I turn to Cal, who has followed me.
"I'm sorry, I've got to . . ."

"I know. You've got to go after him."

135

I find the Fiesta parked down by the boat dock.
Dave is sitting on the hood, messing with his phone.

"Dave!" I yell,
running down the slippery hillside of frozen grass.
"What you saw, that wasn't what you think."

Slowly, slowly, he turns to look at me.
"No? I thought you'd decided to stop mucking up your attendance record.
Instead you cut a whole day of school and . . ."

I stop running.
Dave slides off his car into the muddy sand,
stares at the space in between us.
"After my parents split and we moved across town,
I felt like I didn't measure up anymore.
Then the babies came.
Dad told me he couldn't keep saving for my college.
Andy Bouchard doesn't owe me anything,
even if he does have the cash.

So what was the point of working at school, friendships . . .
dreams? I just let go.
Then, last summer, I had to drive my stepmom
and the babies to the pediatrician.
In the waiting room, I saw you: front page of the *Jasper Weekly*
in a dorktastic white shirt, black ribbon tie.
You'd been chosen for the Honor Band of America
for the second time. Amazing!
But all my stepmom could talk about
was the gossip she'd heard about Steven."

The break in his voice makes me tremble
more than the wind whipping my uncombed hair,
drafting through my thin sweatshirt.

"You were so brave, despite everything, playing on.
I realized what I'd lost by giving up.
So I started trying again, learning programming
from YouTube videos and library books.
Got way too familiar with that egg chair.
Then school started and I wanted to be near you,
like it was the next step."

"This isn't kindergarten, Dave.
I couldn't save my brother, my own family.
Can't even help Cal find a place to stay for next semester."

He looks up sharply at the name.
"He's a great musician, Dave, that's all.
We're music friends."

He snorts, but takes a step closer.
"I think he wouldn't mind if it were more."

"Stop it! You just need to know
that I can't fix anything for anybody.
I don't want people asking me to try."

"What *do* you want, Daisy-brains?"

I am frozen now but not from cold.
Can I get away with a platitude, something I want
that all of Jasper already knows—
like making Honor Band again?
I look at his cynical eyes: He's still picturing me
in Cal's clutches, laughing, spinning.

"I want . . .
a real family."

He grins, sloshes up the beach to meet me
on the hillside of fall-brown grass,

kicking mud off his Timberland boots
as he reaches my side.

"Don't we all? And I can't put one in your life.
But I can show you a pretend one."
He pulls out his cell phone and hits a few keys.
"It's an app I built called Fake Happy Families.
See, you can put your family's faces
into these idyllic settings—
all wearing Santa hats round a tree,
everybody burying Dad in Hawaiian ocean sand . . ."

It's coolly ironic, badass Dave all around.
I want to try it, except
all our family photos show Mom looking miserable,
Dad angry,
Steven gazing away,
and I know the game might make me cry.

"It's amazing, Dave.
You really did teach yourself programming."

"Sometimes you just need someone to inspire you."

"I'm nobody's inspiration.
Sometimes I think my heart is as messed up as Steven's.

I just can't feel; don't think I can love."

"You love to play trumpet," Dave says.

I nod. I do.
No matter what, I do.

"But you can't just put your heart in your music
and wait for people to love you.
You have to put it somewhere else, too.
You have to ask for love."

His voice is tentative.
I think he's as afraid as I am
to unleash secrets into the chill lakeside air of Jasper.

"I want . . . I am asking you . . .
to help me," I say.

And he grins and wraps me in his arms
and kisses me, hard, on the lips.

"I'm taking you back to school."

"Maybe you should come with me.
Maybe show Mr. Angelli that app," I say.

"Now who's being parental?" Dave teases.

We leave the Fiesta by the water
and drive together to Evergreen High.

136

I turn on my stereo,
let the car fill with the sounds of jazz.
I could dance, disappear into every note:
"So What"—the first track from *Kind of Blue*—
telling me, like it always does, to reach, to try, to go on.

"Miles Davis wasn't just about his music," I tell Dave.
"He was about his musicians,
the people he talked with through sound.
He chose people who would challenge him.
Make him better."

He slides his hand along the back of my neck.
His fingers tangle into my hair.
"Like you make me."

137

The grief of loss—

from divorce,
from sending away your only brother,
from running from a future you don't want,
from trying to find hope, a dream,
after everyone gives up on you—

isn't something that goes away.
It just evolves.

You have to return to whatever life you have left,
even if your ears cringe at the unaccustomed blare
of a normal-volume alarm clock
rousing you from bed in the morning;
even if your well-trained lungs struggle to fill with air,
or your body aches.

138

Dave waits, a little possessively, in the egg chair
while Cal and I complete our project
in the study room nearby.

Jeremy has become the son of a slave woman
and her red-haired master.
He has freckles, like Justine's, over his nose
and a mute brother.
He is growing into our lives,
and we talk about him like we see him
standing in the study room before us.

"So, it'll be all of a piece. Our slave, Jeremy,
on his first free Thanksgiving Day,
the first Thanksgiving Day since Lincoln declared it."
Cal scribbles furiously onto a yellow notepad.

"I think there should be some 'before.'"
I page through the books we've piled onto the table.
"Some explanation of the life he left."

Cal nods. "And the after—
what he hopes freedom will bring."
His eyes get that faraway look
that tells me he's missing his little brother.

"Let's give our slave a big dream. A big future."

139

Justine and Ned
and Dave
come for dinner at my house.

It feels surreal, all of us sitting around the table,
with forks and knives.
Mom has even put out real glass tumblers
and flowers in the middle.
Dad helps her set the fancy ceramic tureen on a trivet,
fills our salad plates from the serving bowl.

We eat spicy black bean soup,
pungent with cilantro,
topped with crispy, organic corn tortilla chips,
and nobody minds the exotic smells,
the sound of crunching,
or the laughter.

We are a little cramped, six around the table,
but no one moves to the island.

"This feels like Thanksgiving!" I say.

"Better food, though. I hate turkey," Dave adds,
with a nod of praise at my mother.

She dabs her linen napkin to her face
to hide her flattered smile.
Her eyes still flash the bewildered expression
she wore home from Holland House,
guilty to feel happiness, relief,
yet happy, relieved nonetheless.
Gratified by Dave's compliment,
yet wishing, somehow,
to also be serving mac and cheese,
to be collecting pictures of a household of four
for her scrapbooks.

"Don't expect me to cook like that, Dave.
I make music, not soup."
I struggle to amuse her, mock a menacing fist,
then stop, let my fingers unfurl.
The memory of real violence in this kitchen is too close,
too clear.

Justine reaches across the table, squeezes my hand.
Changes topics in her imperious yet magical way.

"I've found two pink dresses
for the Black-and-White Dance.
I couldn't decide which I liked best, so I bought both.
I'll return whichever one I don't wear.
Maybe you could come over this week and help me choose.
It's less than two weeks away."

"It's good you never asked Cal O'Casey," Ned comments
in his size-enormous-foot-in-mouth, Jasper-nosy way
that I only tolerate because I adore Justine.
"I hear he's gotta go back to Ireland."

"Why?" Dave asks.

"Mrs. Ackerman is pregnant, on bed rest,
and she and Mr. Ackerman can't handle a houseguest
much longer."

"Oh, the poor Ackermans," Mom says.
"I'll whip up a nice pie to bring over to them tomorrow."

"It's a shame," I say,
despite Dave's look of
I-know-she-said-they-were-music-friends-but-
I'm-seething-with-jealousy,
which doesn't exactly make me sad.

"He's an amazing saxophone player. Even Aggie says so.
You should hear him on the bari."

"He must be good," Mom says. "We all know
Daisy isn't one to throw compliments around."

"He's that talented?" Dad asks.

"Enough to help us win Battle of the Bands in the spring,
if he could find a new place to stay," I tell him.

In the long beat that follows,
Justine glares at Ned,
Dave stares curiously at me,
Mom looks confused,
and Dad clears his throat.

Then my nearly-silent-since-he-sent-Steven-away father
speaks.
His voice sounds a little soft but decisive, matter-of-fact.
"Maybe this—Cal's his name, right?—
maybe this Cal fellow could stay here next semester.
We've got an empty room."

"But the Holland House people said that soon,
Steven might be able to come home for visits,"

Mom jumps in.

"Cal could sleep on the family room couch then.
Doubt he'd mind.
And Daisy and Evergreen High can win that band battle.
We can talk to Mr. Orson about it tomorrow."

What words follow that?

Under the table, I pull Dave's hand onto my knee,
lean my head on his shoulder.

Nobody quite knows what to say,
except my mother:
"I made peach upside-down cake
and homemade whipped cream.
Anyone still hungry?"

140

After Ned and Justine have said their good-byes,
Dave and I move to the family room.
The television is tuned to HBO,
where a movie starlet is slipping out of her dress.
Blushing, I turn the television off,
pretty sure now that cable doesn't have all the answers
about love;
ready to be a real girl, with a real boyfriend,
to make my own heat.

I drop beside him on the couch.

"I'm not crazy about Cal O'Casey
being your roommate," Dave says.

"His dad wants him to leave America, give up on his dream.
I—we—know how terrible that feels.
We can't let that happen.
Besides, you can trust me."

"Oh, I trust you. It's *him* . . ."

I laugh and plant a kiss on his nose.
"Don't worry, Dave.
My parents are experts at watching people,
and I couldn't handle a complicated house.
I'm still getting used to feeling safe,
not having to ask permission to stay late
after school . . ."

"Well, I have something to ask you," Dave says.
He scratches his head
until his hair goes from gorgeous to insanely goofy,
then takes my hands in his.
"I don't have the money to rent a tux or anything, but
would you be my date to the Black-and-White Dance?"

I jump onto his lap like that night in the Fiesta,
run my fingers through his mane to set the goofy right.
I can meet Dave at the pits, have him take me to a dance,
kiss him knowing that my being out at night won't
imprison Mom in our house,
that I won't spend the hours afraid
that my parents are fighting,
that, maybe, they'll be watching the clock,
waiting for me to get home on time.
They're only a hallway away now, still,

I kiss my boyfriend's warm mouth
with all the relief and longing
of a hallelujah because,
"Dave, I'd really like to be that."

141

I peek through the closed curtain
of the Evergreen High stage.
My parents sit in the dead-center seats of the third row.
Mom in her faux fur coat;
Dad's leather jacket is on her lap.
They are turned toward each other, talking.
I wish I could see them smile, touch,
but content myself with the closeness of their faces;
try to get used to the fact that they are here
at my school concert.

Justine and Ned are in the audience, too,
fingers entangled, giggling and whispering.
I don't see Dave, but being with me
hasn't magically turned him
into an on-time kind of guy.

"Let's get seated, everybody," Mr. Orson says.
He is wearing a red tie and Santa Claus hat.
The rest of us are in our concert black—skirts, slacks, ties.
I have succumbed to the rules and am wearing black pumps.

I take my seat on one of the folding chairs,
arranged on risers for the occasion.
The curtain opens.

We begin with "Adeste Fideles"
("O Come, All Ye Faithful").
The steady, rich tones of the baritone sax
embrace me with the sound of comfort,
carry me through my fight against memories
of baby Steven, of toddler Steven,
still not dangerous, still just odd.

The audience applauds.
As I shuffle my sheet music for the next number,
I catch a glimpse of Mom's beaming face.

Then we play the swing medley,
the Ellington piece.

Dave must have slipped in the back with Aggie
sometime during "Good King Wenceslas,"
because I see them
when we all stand up to acknowledge applause.

And it's my turn.

I lay my fingers over the valves,
raise my horn to my lips,
test the mouthpiece,
then nod to Mr. Orson,
who signals the accompanist to begin
"Hallelujah."
And I reach the music out, out into the audience
to Aggie,
who loves to hear me play;
to my parents,
who are trying to learn how to treat me like a child again;
to Justine,
who never quit on me;
to Ned,
because he belongs to Justine;
to Dave,
who has decided to try to become
the kind of man we imagined him being
those years ago making sandcastles and flying on swings.

And I will help him.

The standing ovation brings tears to my eyes,
and I don't care if Jasper notices my smudged mascara
as I wipe them away.

In the lobby afterward,
cookies and bottled water are proffered,
"Band Geeks Rock" fund-raiser T-shirts sold.

"You sounded great, Cal," I say.

"You too. A fun first American band concert," he says.
"But not my last, thanks to your family."

142

Saturday, I wake up to falling snow.
I wonder what Steven is doing
as I drive slowly into town,
whether the people at Holland House know
how to prepare his waffles;
imagine him being gentled into his coat for a walk;
chuckle at my knowledge that he'll refuse to wear a hat;
feel tears spring to my eyes.

My life feels like a book with a chunk taken out of the
middle, moving from one bizarre planet
to another with no journey in between:
all change, no transition,
what Mr. Orson would surely deem a bad composition.

I don't know what else to do
but go on:
back down the stairs to the kitchen,
back to school and jazz band,
back to the parking lot of the Arts Center,
where I park in a covered spot, grab my trumpet case,

head for the Youth Orchestra practice room.

Sometimes my trumpet roars like a lion
with a splinter removed from its paw.
Sometimes it whispers the covert celebration
of a nameless slave set free.
And sometimes it wails like a grief-stricken sister
who has lost her brother.

When the rehearsal is over,
I pack up my trumpet quickly,
try to look casual as I wander to the woodwind section.
Shelby is still methodically wiping down her flute.

"Hi, Shelby. I was wondering, since we both live in Jasper,
if you'd ever like to ride over here with me.
I, uh, have a car."

"I do, too." Her voice is the slightest bit taut, mechanical.
"My dad gave me one for my sixteenth birthday.
It is very large, safe. Hard to park."
She gives a tentative grin.

I smile back. "Dads are very protective.
Anyway, if your car is ever in the shop or anything,
I can drive."

"Me too. I mean, same thing for you.
If your car breaks down."
She looks a little breathless, uncertain,
waiting, perhaps, for a dialogue she's practiced,
even dreamed about.
I cannot walk away.

"That sounds great.
We musicians need to stick together.
Like family."

And now I do have to go;
my lesson is in ten minutes.
But one day, maybe,
I'll invite Shelby out for Thai food after practice,
ask her how she started playing the flute,
tell her my story.

143

The gossip's spread round Jasper, of course:
that the Irish boy is moving in with the Meehan family
now that they've given up on that disabled child.

And I hate it when Andy Bouchard gives me a free coffee
and a hang-in-there nudge; hate it less
when Shirley presses me against her ample bosom
and says, "It's okay to cry, my little Daisy,"
or when Mrs. Ackerman calls to thank my mom for the pie
and for giving Cal, "that charming boy,"
a way to stay in America.

"I'm all packed up and ready for tonight's move-in!"
Cal announces as he sits on the cafeteria bench
across from me and Dave.

And I don't hate it at all when Ashleigh Anderson pauses
not too far from our table, takes in me beside Dave,
across from my new housemate, Cal,
and maybe looks a little bit jealous.

I pick up my fork,
dig into the slightly disgusting bliss of turkey and gravy.

"Seriously, Daisy,
you shouldn't look like you enjoy that so much,"
Justine says, as she and Ned join us.
He's carrying trays for both of them: two salads.

"She's got a right to like whatever she likes."
Ned, of all people, comes to my defense.

144

There's pain in my mother's face
as she watches Cal carry his few boxes of clothes,
books, instruments, up our stairs;
stands silently in Steven's bedroom doorway
while Cal puts his underwear, his shirts,
in my brother's emptied dresser drawers.

"Take your time settling in."
Her voice is barely above a whisper.
"We'll have dinner in an hour."

"Thank you, Mrs. Meehan. I'm so very grateful to you."
I see the tiniest charmed-by-the-Irish twinkle
in my mom's wistful eyes.

I follow her downstairs to the living room.
We both drop onto the couch.
"Dave's coming for dinner, too," I tell her.
"To keep watch on me. Or maybe he just likes your pie."

I pull out my phone, smile

at the custom Fake Happy Families screen saver
Dave has made, with his and my faces superimposed
on a "prom night" photo booth cartoon.
Beneath my real kohl-lined eyes, I am adorned
in flowing pink satin, toes peeping from beneath the frills
in black-and-blue Keds.
Dave's messy brown hair, easy smile, hover
over the most ordinary jeans and tee.
But wrapped around the neck of his hoodie
is a huge purple bow tie.

"My goodness, this house is always overflowing these days."
Her tone is bright,
but there's an odd hesitation in the way she speaks.
She's thinking, perhaps,
of this morning's call from Holland House,
asking to approve a new medication regimen
to try to moderate the violence
that comes with Steven's anxiety.

I think maybe the house is too loud for my mother.

"I miss him, Mom," is all I can think to say.

"Me, too." She wraps her bony arms around me.
She says nothing more. Doesn't move.
Doesn't let me go.

We're still there on the couch
when Dad gets home right after work
without stopping at the gym.

"Gonna go to yoga tonight, hon?"
he asks, kicking off his shoes, tugging at his tie.
He looks older somehow,
even though there are fewer tight lines around his mouth.

"I dunno." Mom's arms slide away from me now.
She stands up, goes to his side.
"Maybe we could have wine with dinner? Light candles?
Put on some music?"

They stand together in the living room doorway.
I sit alone on the couch. Free from Steven
but no longer joined to my mom and dad
as a third parent.
I have lost my place in this house,
but maybe that's how it needs to be.

I bury my hurt in this idea:
that, maybe, it's just time.

"Or I could play something," I say.

145

"Whatcha doin'?" Cal asks.

I'm surprised.
I'd somehow managed to forget
there was another teenager in this house
who, clothes unpacked, books sorted,
could come down the stairs unbidden, say hello.

"I was going to play something. You could join me.
Improvise a little."

"Hang on."
He's back in moments with his saxophone.

I press my lips against familiar cold metal,
feel the rush of belonging as I fill my lungs
and breathe out
into the song that's been building in my heart
through these icy weeks,
into the music that is Steven scratching and whirling,
pounding and slapping

from inside the metal confines of his mind;
push the notes:
seemingly random yet completely rational
gusts of expression, communication, reaching
for the world outside—the listener
jabbing and rocking and softly humming—
shouting and singing and wildly scatting,
making meaning where before there was chaos.

The tips of my overgrown bangs
dip into the wet of my tears.
My fingers, forehead moisten with sweat.
I fight the slipperiness, press the valves firmly,
play the love, the hate,
the misery, the hope,
the freedom that I wanted, never wanted, can't have;
that doesn't exist.

I play the music of Steven
for Steven;
ragged, helpless,
it owns me, envelops me
with an incomprehensible love—

I almost don't notice when Cal picks up the tune,
but suddenly he's there, brightening the minor keys,

adding those daring deep notes he plays so well.

Our duet rambles imperfectly,
awkward as my parents holding hands,
Cal's phone calls to his father,
but certain in its way.
Strong.

It's the start of something loud and soft,
classic jazz and wordless love song,
free and entangled:
forgiving yourself for being human,
for the things you want to grab hold of, own,
and giving yourself permission
when you need
to let go.

Acknowledgments

Carrie Harris, Elana Johnson, Jessi Kirby and Gretchen McNeil: silly, salty, cynical and matchless pillars of writerly support. Conrad Wesselhoeft, Cathy Benson, Megan Bilder, Louise Spiegler and Susan Greenway, in whose critique group this story had its start. The team at Penguin, beginning with my amazing editor, Kendra Levin, copyeditors Ryan Sullivan and Abigail Powers, designers Vanessa Han and Jim Hoover, and Viking's literary leader, Ken Wright, for shepherding another verse novel to publication. My awesome agent, Catherine Drayton. The people who helped guide my research: Kyla Moscovich and Natalie Dungey, trumpet girls extraordinaire; Chris Coleman, PhD, Colleen Peck, MD and Carol Kirk, early autism information resources; and the countless individuals who shared their stories of living with developmentally disabled family members. For vetting the finished manuscript: Alexandra Watters, Autism Speaks, and Tonia Ferguson, The Autism Society. And my family, for their encouragement and support despite my myriad shortcomings as a daughter, wife and mother in the hours I spend trying to be a writer.